卡里·紀伯倫 ——————————————— 著
（Kahlil Gibran，1883 ～ 1931）

生於黎巴嫩北部臨海的貝什里村（Bsharri）。此地孕育了基
督與腓尼基文明，也是蘇美人愛與豐饒女神伊絲塔所居之
地。豐富的宗教氣息與東方文化，使得他的詩作能在西方浪
漫主義的精神上，更添東方神祕主義的靈性色彩。
紀伯倫一生顛沛流離、年少痛失至親，1908 年又因發表小
說《叛逆的靈魂》觸怒黎巴嫩當局，遭到放逐。即使飽嘗磨
難，他仍筆耕不輟，1923 年出版的《先知》即是他十多部
作品集大成之作，甫出版即轟動世界文壇。他將 40 多年
來的人生閱歷，精煉成《先知》中 28 篇綻放著永恆智慧光
芒的散文詩，以溫潤、豁達的話語撫慰因愛情、工作、生死
而感到焦躁不安的人們。

趙永芬 —————————————————— 譯

畢業於美國德州大學奧斯汀分校及東海大學外文系，自小愛
讀小說，長大以後愛上小說翻譯。盼望未來持續翻譯更多優
秀的作品，以饗讀者。

先知

綻放愛與哲思之美的
不朽散文詩集

The Prophet

卡里 紀伯倫 ———— 著　趙永芬 ———— 譯

Kahlil Gibran

紀伯倫的作品像一個飽經滄桑的老人，講述為人處世的哲理，於平靜中流露出淡淡的悲涼。

——中國作家　冰心

紀伯倫是最早從東方揚起的風暴，他橫掃西方，為西海岸帶來了鮮花。

——美國總統　羅斯福

世界將從這位黎巴嫩天才身上看到很多東西，他是二十世紀的威廉·布萊克。

——法國雕塑大師　羅丹

如果某個男人或女人讀了這本書，無法安靜地接受這位偉人的哲學，心中無法歡唱著來自內心深處的樂章，那麼這個男人或女人，就生命和真理而言，他們確實已經死亡。

——《芝加哥郵報》

真理就在這裡，《先知》以黎巴嫩式的美、音樂和理念表達真理。這是一本小聖經，讓那些準備接受真理的人去閱讀，去迷戀。

——《芝加哥晚報》

《先知》具有東方蘇菲精神，闡述了許多高尚且富有哲理的教誨，文筆輕柔優美，如潺潺流水，有迷人的音樂感。

——黎巴嫩著名文學史家 漢納·法胡里

傳承一代又一代的經典

記得小學時在父親的書架上看到一冊精裝燙金的紀伯倫全集，偷偷拿下來翻閱，第一篇就是《先知》，看了幾頁，看不懂，就又放回書架上。

等到自己大學後，平裝版薄薄的《先知》隨著我四處遷移，始終是擺放在書桌旁，最常翻閱的那一格書架上。

前一陣子，在女兒房間裡聊天時，瞥見她書桌上也擺了一本《先知》，她買的是中英對照的版本。

這本出版將近一百年的書，就這樣在一代又一代的年輕人之間流傳著，也印證了經典書籍的豐富與永恆，不受一時流行的興衰而改變。《先知》就像是一位擁有豐富生命經驗的長者，向迷惘徬徨或者好奇興奮的年輕人，敘說著人生的種種。

其實這種「過來人」的道德教訓很不討好，因為聽得懂的，你不必說，他早就懂了；聽不懂的，你再怎麼說，他也無法體會。而且真正有用的生命經驗，說起來無非也都是老生常談而已，那麼，為什麼《先知》這本書會感動一代又一代的年輕人呢？

我想，大概是因為《先知》是用詩的形式來說這些人生道理。

詩除了是最精練的語言文字，還有幾個特性。通常語言是具有邏輯性的，是理性的，而相對於語言的音樂則是感性的，屬於非邏輯性的。但是，詩介於兩者之間，因為詩不只是文字語言的組合，它還具有音樂的韻律。

的確，詩的外在形式，即詩的分行，就具有音樂上的節奏感。同時最重要的是，詩有其獨特的意象，詩是音樂、故事敘述以及繪畫這三種藝術的結合。在讀詩的時候，我們的腦海中不只用理性思考，還動用了各種感官形成的想像。

　　比如就有詩人說，玫瑰不是詩，玫瑰的香氣才是詩；天空不是詩，天光才是詩；海不是詩，海的浪潮才是詩。因此，詩必須在想像中動用到我們的視覺、嗅覺以及聽覺。

　　這些感官的經驗，是普世共通的，也是我們過往生命經驗中難以忘懷的，所以會烙印在我們的記憶裡。紀伯倫的《先知》用一個又一個生動的意象，呈現出理性邏輯的道德教訓，再輔以詩精練的文字，所以其中許多句子已經成為各個國家、世代經常傳誦的金句，甚至成為成語了。

　　記得多年前有一部電影《春風化雨》（Dead Poets Society），電影中的國文老師在教學生有關於「詩」的用途時，有段非常棒的解說：「我們不是因為詩可愛，才作詩或讀詩。想讀詩、想作詩，是因為我們是人類，而人類是充滿熱情的。醫學、法律、企業、工程，這些都是崇高的職業，而人們也賴以為生。但是詩、美麗、浪漫、愛，這才是人活著的原因。同學們，人類生命的戲劇仍在上演，而你們都能為此獻出一篇詩！」

　　是的，生命是無拘無束、湧向四面八方的熱情，是對這個世界最狂野的愛，而詩詞文學就是我們對生命的獻詩與頌歌。

　　因此，這本結合了詩歌文學與生命經驗的經典，應該還會出現在一代又一代的年輕人桌上。

李偉文

牙醫師・作家・環保志工

第1章

船來了

The Coming of the Ship

我已準備動身，帆已張滿，
殷殷盼望海風吹起。
只要再吸一口這靜止的空氣，
只要再回首投以依戀的一睹，
我就會與你們為伍，成為其中一名水手。

Ready am I to go,
and my eagerness with sails full set awaits the wind.
Only another breath will I breathe in this still air,
only another loving look cast backward.
And then I shall stand among you, a seafarer among seafarers.

阿穆斯塔法是當代的曙光，集萬千榮寵於一身。他在歐法里斯城等了十二個寒暑，等待他的船返航，載他回到出生的小島。

到了第十二年，在收割月的第七天，
他登上城牆外的山丘朝海眺望，
看見他的船乘著薄霧而來。
他的心扉霍然敞開，
他的喜悅飛到遙遠的海上。
然後他閉上眼睛，在沉靜的靈魂中默禱。

然而他走下山時，哀傷卻湧上心頭，
他想：
我怎能平靜離去而不悲傷？
不，我將離開這座城市，難免感到心痛。
在這座城裡，我度過漫長痛苦的白晝，
也捱過孤獨的漫漫長夜，
誰能揮別痛苦與孤獨而了無遺憾？

在這些街道上，我曾撒落太多心靈的碎片，
在山野之間，
許多心愛的孩子也曾赤裸走過，
我無法與他們分離，而不感到沉重與傷痛。

Almustafa, the chosen and the beloved, who was a dawn unto his own day, had waited twelve years in the city of Orphalese for his ship that was to return and bear him back to the isle of his birth.

And in the twelfth year, on the seventh day of Ielool, the month of reaping, he climbed the hill without the city walls and looked seaward; and he beheld his ship coming with the mist.

Then the gates of his heart were flung open,

and his joy flew far over the sea.

And he closed his eyes and prayed in the silences of his soul.

But as he descended the hill, a sadness came upon him,

and he thought in his heart:

How shall I go in peace and without sorrow?

Nay, not without a wound in the spirit shall I leave this city.

Long were the days of pain I have spent within its walls,

and long were the nights of aloneness;

and who can depart from his pain and his aloneness without regret?

Too many fragments of the spirit have I scattered in these streets,

and too many are the children of my longing

that walk naked among these hills,

and I cannot withdraw from them without a burden and an ache.

今天我不是褪下一件衣物，

而是親手撕裂自己的皮膚。

我拋諸身後的也不是一個念頭，

而是一顆因飢渴變得甜蜜的心。

但我不能再耽擱了。

召喚萬物的大海此刻也召喚著我，

我非登船不可。

因若是留下，縱使生命在夜晚燃燒不輟，

我也終會凍結僵化，被囚禁在鑄模之中。

我多麼樂於帶走這一切，

但我怎麼能夠？

脣與舌給了聲音翅膀，聲音卻載不動脣舌，

它必須獨自追尋蒼穹。

孤鷹必須離開窩巢，方能飛越太陽。

此時他已行至山下，

卻又轉頭望向海面。

他望見船駛近港口，

佇立船首的水手，

全都來自他的故鄉。

It is not a garment I cast off this day,

but a skin that I tear with my own hands.

Nor is it a thought I leave behind me,

but a heart made sweet with hunger and with thirst.

Yet I cannot tarry longer.

The sea that calls all things unto her calls me,

and I must embark.

For to stay, though the hours burn in the night,

is to freeze and crystallize and be bound in a mould.

Fain would I take with me all that is here.

But how shall I?

A voice cannot carry the tongue and the lips that give it wings.

Alone must it seek the ether.

And alone and without his nest shall the eagle fly across the sun.

Now when he reached the foot of the hill,

he turned again towards the sea,

and he saw his ship approaching the harbour,

and upon her prow the mariners,

the men of his own land.

他的靈魂向他們呼喊：
我先人的子孫，乘風破浪的人啊，
你們在我夢中航行了多少次，
而今，你們在我清醒時翩然來到，
這才是我更深沉的夢境。

我已準備動身，
帆已張滿，殷殷盼望海風吹起。
只要再吸一口這靜止的空氣，
只要再回首投以依戀的一睹，
我就會與你們為伍，成為其中一名水手。

而你，浩瀚的大海，不眠的母親，
河川和溪流只有奔向你，才能得到平靜與自由，
只等這條溪再繞一個彎，
只待林間再一聲低吟，
我就會奔向你，
像是無拘無束的水滴，奔向無垠大海。

他走著走著，看見遠處的男男女女
走出田地和葡萄園，匆匆趕向城門。
他也聽見他們呼喊他的名字，
從這塊田喊到那畝地，爭相走告他的船來了。

And his soul cried out to them, and he said:

Sons of my ancient mother, you riders of the tides,

How often have you sailed in my dreams.

And now you come in my awakening,

which is my deeper dream.

Ready am I to go,

and my eagerness with sails full set awaits the wind.

Only another breath will I breathe in this still air,

only another loving look cast backward,

And then I shall stand among you, a seafarer among seafarers.

And you, vast sea, sleepless mother,

Who alone are peace and freedom to the river and the stream,

Only another winding will this stream make,

only another murmur in this glade,

And then I shall come to you,

a boundless drop to a boundless ocean.

And as he walked he saw from afar men and women leaving their

fields and their vineyards and hastening towards the city gates.

And he heard their voices calling his name,

and shouting from field to field telling one another of the coming of

his ship.

於是他問自己：

離別之日莫非就是相聚之日？

難道我的黃昏實際上是我的黎明？

我該拿什麼給拋下犁具、

停止榨酒來見我的人？

我的心能化作一棵結實纍纍的大樹，

讓我採下果子送給他們嗎？

我的想望能像湧泉一般，盛滿他們的水杯嗎？

我可以成為一座豎琴，讓全能之手撥弄嗎？

或成為一支蘆笛，任由祂的氣息吹進我的身體？

我尋求寧靜，

而我在寧靜中找到什麼寶物，

可以信心滿滿地贈予別人？

若說今天是我的豐收日，我曾在哪塊田地撒下了種子？

又是在哪個不復記憶的季節撒下的呢？

若說此刻是我高舉油燈之時，

燃燒其中的火焰也不是我點燃的。

我舉起的油燈空虛又漆黑，

是守夜人為它注滿燈油，

並且點亮油燈。

And he said to himself:

Shall the day of parting be the day of gathering?

And shall it be said that my eve was in truth my dawn?

And what shall I give unto him who has left his plough in mid-furrow, or to him who has stopped the wheel of his winepress?

Shall my heart become a tree heavy-laden with fruit that I may gather and give unto them?

And shall my desires flow like a fountain that I may fill their cups?

Am I a harp that the hand of the mighty may touch me,

or a flute that his breath may pass through me?

A seeker of silences am I,

and what treasure have I found in silences

that I may dispense with confidence?

If this is my day of harvest, in what fields have I sowed the seed,

and in what unremembered seasons?

If this indeed be the hour in which I lift up my lantern,

it is not my flame that shall burn therein.

Empty and dark shall I raise my lantern,

And the guardian of the night shall fill it with oil

and he shall light it also.

他口中說著這些，
但心中還有許多話沒說，
因為他說不出心底的祕密。

他一走進城裡，大家都前去迎接，
他們齊聲向他呼喊。
城裡長老走上前說：
請先別離開我們。
在我們的遲暮之年，你就像正午的陽光，
你的青春讓我們有夢可做。
你不是陌生人，也不是過客，
你是我們的子弟，我們摯愛的人。
請別讓我們的眼睛因渴望見到你而痠痛。

男祭司和女祭司對他說：
別讓大海的波浪就此將我們分離，
別讓你和我們共度的時光成為回憶。
你的精神早已與我們同行，
你的身影是照在我們臉上的光芒。
我們多麼愛你，
但我們的愛像被面紗蒙住，說不出口。
此時它卻向你高喊，
並願展現在你面前。

These things he said in words.

But much in his heart remained unsaid.

For he himself could not speak his deeper secret.

And when he entered into the city all the people came to meet him,

and they were crying out to him as with one voice.

And the elders of the city stood forth and said:

Go not yet away from us.

A noontide have you been in our twilight,

and your youth has given us dreams to dream.

No stranger are you among us, nor a guest,

but our son and our dearly beloved.

Suffer not yet our eyes to hunger for your face.

And the priests and the priestesses said unto him:

Let not the waves of the sea separate us now,

and the years you have spent in our midst become a memory.

You have walked among us a spirit,

and your shadow has been a light upon our faces.

Much have we loved you.

But speechless was our love, and with veils has it been veiled.

Yet now it cries aloud unto you,

and would stand revealed before you.

從來，只有到分離的時刻，

才知道愛得多深。

其他人也過來懇求他。

他卻不回答，只是低頭，

身旁的人看見淚水滴落他的胸膛。

他和眾人一起走向神廟前的大廣場。

一個女人走出聖殿，

她名叫艾蜜特拉，是個預言家。

他用無比溫柔的眼光看著她，

因為他到這座城的第一天，

就是她最先尋找他，並且相信他。

她向他行禮，然後說：

神的先知啊，為了追求至高無上的道理，

你已經走過迢迢長路，尋找你的船。

如今船已抵達，而你必須離去。

你深深渴望返回記憶之地，

前往深切渴望的居所；

我們的愛不能束縛你，

我們的需要也不能攔阻你。

And ever has it been that love knows not its own depth until the hour of separation.

And others came also and entreated him.
But he answered them not. He only bent his head;
and those who stood near saw his tears falling upon his breast.
And he and the people proceeded towards the great square before the temple.

And there came out of the sanctuary a woman whose name was Almitra. And she was a seeress.
And he looked upon her with exceeding tenderness,
for it was she who had first sought and believed in him when he had been but a day in their city.

And she hailed him, saying:
Prophet of God, in quest of the uttermost,
long have you searched the distances for your ship.
And now your ship has come, and you must needs go.
Deep is your longing for the land of your memories
and the dwelling-place of your greater desires;
and our love would not bind you
nor our needs hold you.

但在你離開我們之前，

請對我們說些話，把你的真理說給我們聽。

我們將把真理傳給我們的子女，

他們再傳給他們的子女，

於是真理將永不滅絕。

你曾孤獨守望我們的白晝，

也曾在不眠之際，

傾聽我們睡眠中的哭泣和歡笑。

現在，請讓我們看清自己，

告訴我們你在生死之間看透的一切。

於是他回答：

歐法里斯的人們啊，

除了此刻在你們靈魂中湧動的念頭之外，

我還能告訴你們什麼呢？

Yet this we ask ere you leave us,

that you speak to us and give us of your truth.

And we will give it unto our children,

and they unto their children,

and it shall not perish.

In your aloneness you have watched with our days,

and in your wakefulness you have listened to the weeping and the

laughter of our sleep.

Now therefore disclose us to ourselves,

and tell us all that has been shown you of that which is between birth

and death.

And he answered:

People of Orphalese,

of what can I speak save of that which is even now moving within

your souls?

第 2 章

愛

On Love

愛只付出自己，也只犧牲自己。
愛不是占有，也無人能據為己有。
因為愛就是圓滿自足。

Love gives naught but itself and takes naught but from itself.
Love possesses not nor would it be possessed;
For love is sufficient unto love.

艾 蜜特拉說，跟我們說說「愛」吧。
他抬起頭，看著眾人，

人們悄然無聲。
他大聲說道：

當愛情召喚你，跟隨它，
即使它的路途艱險又陡峭。

當愛的翅膀擁抱你，順從它，
即使它藏在翼梢的利劍可能傷了你。

當愛情對你說話，相信它，
即使它的聲音可能粉碎你的夢，
如同北風將花園吹得荒蕪。

因為愛為你加冕時，也能把你釘上十字架。
它呵護你的成長時，也會修剪你的枝葉。
它爬上你的梢頭、
輕撫你在陽光下微微顫動的嫩枝時，
也會伏在你的根部，
搖晃緊抓泥土的樹根。

T hen said Almitra, "Speak to us of Love."
And he raised his head and looked upon the people,
and there fell a stillness upon them.
And with a great voice he said:

When love beckons to you, follow him,
Though his ways are hard and steep.

And When his wings enfold you yield to him,
Though the sword hidden among his pinions may wound you.

And When he speaks to you believe in him,
Though his voice may shatter your dreams as the north wind lays
waste the garden.

For even as love crowns you so shall he crucify you.
Even as he is for your growth so is he for your pruning.
Even as he ascends to your height and caresses your tenderest
branches that quiver in the sun,
So shall he descend to your roots and shake them in their clinging to
the earth.

愛採集你，好比收割麥穀。

愛鞭打你，使你赤身露體。

愛將你過篩，使你脫去穀殼。

愛將你磨成潔白的麵粉，

揉捏你，直至你成為柔軟的麵糰。

然後將你放進它神聖的火焰中，

使你成為聖餐中的聖餅。

愛會對你做這些事，

使你明白自我心靈的祕密，

進而成為生命本質的一部分。

但是，如果恐懼使你只願追尋愛的平靜與歡愉，

那倒不如遮掩你的赤裸，

離開愛的打穀場，

走入四季不分的世界。在那裡，

你將歡笑，但無法盡興，

你將流淚，卻無法盡情哭泣。

愛只付出自己，也只犧牲自己。

愛不是占有，也無人能據為己有。

因為愛就是圓滿自足。

Like sheaves of corn he gathers you unto himself.

He threshes you to make you naked.

He sifts you to free you from your husks.

He grinds you to whiteness.

He kneads you until you are pliant;

And then he assigns you to his sacred fire,

that you may become sacred bread for God's sacred feast.

All these things shall love do unto you

that you may know the secrets of your heart,

and in that knowledge become a fragment of Life's heart.

But if in your fear you would seek only love's peace and love's pleasure,

Then it is better for you that you cover your nakedness

and pass out of love's threshing-floor,

Into the seasonless world where you shall laugh,

but not all of your laughter,

and weep, but not all of your tears.

Love gives naught but itself and takes naught but from itself.

Love possesses not nor would it be possessed;

For love is sufficient unto love.

當你愛的時候，
不要說「神在我心中」，
應該說「我在神心中」。

不要以為你可以主導愛的路徑，
因為如果愛認為你值得，
它自然會為你帶路。

愛別無他求，只想圓滿自己。
但如果你心中有愛，又必有渴望，
那就祈求這些吧：

願心柔軟，像奔流的小溪，對著夜晚吟唱它的旋律。
願了解過多溫柔帶來的痛苦。
願自己因領悟愛而受傷，
並且心甘情願地淌血。
願在黎明醒來時心情飛揚，
感謝又有一天可以去愛；
在中午歇息時，冥想愛的狂喜；
在傍晚回家時，滿懷感激之情；
然後在心裡為所愛的人禱告，
並唱著讚美歌，安然入睡。

When you love you should not say,

"God is in my heart,"

but rather, "I am in the heart of God."

And think not you can direct the course of love,

for love, if it finds you worthy,

directs your course.

Love has no other desire but to fulfill itself.

But if you love and must needs have desires,

let these be your desires:

To melt and be like a running brook that sings its melody to the night.

To know the pain of too much tenderness.

To be wounded by your own understanding of love;

And to bleed willingly and joyfully.

To wake at dawn with a winged heart and give thanks for another

day of loving;

To rest at the noon hour and meditate love's ecstasy;

To return home at eventide with gratitude;

And then to sleep with a prayer for the beloved in your heart

and a song of praise upon your lips.

第 3 章

婚姻

On Marriage

請在你們相依的世界中保留些許空間，
讓天堂的微風在你們之間舞動。
彼此相愛，
但不要讓愛成為枷鎖，
讓愛像是你倆靈魂海岸之間流動的海洋。

But let there be spaces in your togetherness.
And let the winds of the heavens dance between you.
Love one another,
but make not a bond of love:
Let it rather be a moving sea between the shores of your souls.

然後，艾蜜特拉又問，大師，那麼「婚姻」呢？他回答說：

你們一起出生，也將終生廝守。
當死亡的白翼撲散你們的生命時，你們仍必相守。
是的，即使在神靜默的記憶裡，你們也將同在。
但是，請在你們相依的世界中保留些許空間，
讓天堂的微風在你們之間舞動。

彼此相愛，但不要讓愛成為枷鎖，
讓愛像是你倆靈魂海岸之間流動的海洋。
斟滿彼此的杯子，但不要同飲一杯。
彼此餵食麵包，但不要同吃一塊。
一起唱歌舞蹈，快樂逍遙，
但也要各自獨處保有自我。
好比魯特琴的琴弦，
雖因同一首樂曲振動，卻是各自獨立。

奉獻你們的心，但不要交由對方保管，
因為只有生命之手才能包容你們的心。
你們要站在一起，但不要靠得太近，
因為柱子必須各自矗立，才足以支撐神殿，
如同橡樹和柏樹無法在彼此的陰影下成長。

Then Almitra spoke again and said, "And what of Marriage, master?" And he answered saying:

You were born together, and together you shall be forevermore.

You shall be together when the white wings of death scatter your days.

Aye, you shall be together even in the silent memory of God.

But let there be spaces in your togetherness.

And let the winds of the heavens dance between you.

Love one another, but make not a bond of love:

Let it rather be a moving sea between the shores of your souls.

Fill each other's cup but drink not from one cup.

Give one another of your bread but eat not from the same loaf.

Sing and dance together and be joyous,

but let each one of you be alone,

Even as the strings of a lute are alone though they quiver with the same music.

Give your hearts, but not into each other's keeping.

For only the hand of Life can contain your hearts.

And stand together yet not too near together:

For the pillars of the temple stand apart,

And the oak tree and the cypress grow not in each other's shadow.

孩子

On Children

你的孩子不是你的，

他們是「生命」的子女，是生命自身的渴望。

他們經你而生，但非出自於你，

他們雖然和你在一起，卻不屬於你。

Your children are not your children.

They are the sons and daughters of Life's longing for itself.

They come through you but not from you.

And though they are with you, yet they belong not to you.

個懷裡抱著嬰兒的婦人說，跟我們說說「孩子」吧。

　　　於是他說：

你的孩子不是你的，

他們是「生命」的子女，是生命自身的渴望。

他們經你而生，但非出自於你，

他們雖然和你在一起，卻不屬於你。

你可以給他們愛，但別把你的思想也給他們，

因為他們有自己的思想。

你的房子可以供他們安身，但無法讓他們的靈魂安住，

因為他們的靈魂住在明日之屋，

那裡你去不了，哪怕是在夢中。

你可以勉強自己變得像他們，但不要想讓他們變得像你。

因為生命不會倒退，也不會駐足於昨日。

你好比一把弓，

孩子是從你身上射出的生命之箭。

弓箭手看見無窮路徑上的箭靶，

於是祂大力拉彎你這把弓，希望祂的箭能射得又快又遠。

欣然屈服在神的手中吧，

因為祂既愛那疾飛的箭，

也愛那穩定的弓。

And a woman who held a babe against her bosom said, "Speak to us of Children." And he said:

Your children are not your children.

They are the sons and daughters of Life's longing for itself.

They come through you but not from you,

And though they are with you, yet they belong not to you.

You may give them your love but not your thoughts,

For they have their own thoughts.

You may house their bodies but not their souls,

For their souls dwell in the house of tomorrow,

which you cannot visit, not even in your dreams.

You may strive to be like them, but seek not to make them like you.

For life goes not backward nor tarries with yesterday.

You are the bows

from which your children as living arrows are sent forth.

The archer sees the mark upon the path of the infinite, and He bends

you with His might that His arrows may go swift and far.

Let your bending in the Archer's hand be for gladness;

For even as He loves the arrow that flies,

so He loves also the bow that is stable.

給予

On Giving

你獻出財產時，其實給予得很少。
你獻出自己時，才是真正的給予。

You give but little when you give of your possessions.
It is when you give of yourself that you truly give.

之後一個富人說，跟我們談談「給予」吧。
他回答說：

你獻出財產時，其實給得很少。
你獻出自己時，才是真正的給予。

財產是什麼？
財產不就是唯恐明天需要而保存與守護的東西嗎？
一隻過分謹慎的狗跟隨朝聖者前去聖城時，
在途中把骨頭埋進無跡可循的沙子裡，
明天究竟能帶給牠什麼呢？

需要的恐懼是什麼？不就是需要本身嗎？
若水井滿了仍害怕口渴，
這種渴如何能夠消解？

有人擁有很多，卻給得很少——
而且他們給予是為了博得讚賞，
這種隱藏的念頭，使得他們的付出美意盡失。

有人擁有極少，卻付出全部。
這些人相信生命，相信生命的慷慨大度，
他們的箱篋永不匱乏。

Then said a rich man, "Speak to us of Giving."
And he answered:

You give but little when you give of your possessions.
It is when you give of yourself that you truly give.

For what are your possessions but things you keep and guard for fear
you may need them tomorrow?
And tomorrow, what shall tomorrow bring to the over-prudent dog
burying bones in the trackless sand as he follows the pilgrims to the
holy city?

And what is fear of need but need itself?
Is not dread of thirst when your well is full,
the thirst that is unquenchable?

There are those who give little of the much which they have –
and they give it for recognition
and their hidden desire makes their gifts unwholesome.

And there are those who have little and give it all.
These are the believers in life and the bounty of life,
and their coffer is never empty.

有人快樂地付出，快樂就是他們的獎賞。

有人痛苦地付出，痛苦就是他們的洗禮。

有人付出時不感覺痛苦，

不尋求快樂，也不懷抱行善的念頭；

他們的給予好比遠處山谷中的桃金孃，

將花香吐入空中。

神透過這些人的手說話，

從他們的眼對大地微笑。

別人開口求你時給予固然好，

若能體恤別人需求，不等對方開口即給予更佳；

對樂善好施的人來說，

尋找接受者比給予更快樂。

你還有什麼東西不想給人嗎？

總有一天，你擁有的一切都得拱手讓人；

不如現在就給吧，

把給予的機會留給自己，而非你的後人。

你常說：「我願意給，但只給受之無愧的人。」

你果園裡的樹不會這麼說，你牧場上的牲口也不會這麼說。

牠們要給予，才能延續生命；

若是不給，就會步上死亡。

There are those who give with joy, and that joy is their reward.

And there are those who give with pain, and that pain is their baptism.

And there are those who give and know not pain in giving,

nor do they seek joy, nor give with mindfulness of virtue;

They give as in yonder valley

the myrtle breathes its fragrance into space.

Through the hands of such as these God speaks,

and from behind their eyes He smiles upon the earth.

It is well to give when asked,

but it is better to give unasked, through understanding;

And to the open-handed

the search for one who shall receive is joy greater than giving.

And is there aught you would withhold?

All you have shall some day be given;

Therefore give now,

that the season of giving may be yours and not your inheritors'.

You often say, "I would give, but only to the deserving."

The trees in your orchard say not so, nor the flocks in your pasture.

They give that they may live,

for to withhold is to perish.

一個值得享有上天賜予畫夜的人，
當然值得你給他的一切。
一個值得啜飲生命之洋的人，
當然值得從你的小溪舀一杯水。

姑且不談慈悲，
還有什麼美德更勝於接受給予的勇氣和信心？
而你是什麼人，
竟要人們撕裂胸膛，揭露自尊，
好讓你看到他們裸裎的價值和無愧的自尊？

你得先讓自己成為夠格的施予者，
和施予的工具。
因為其實是生命施予生命——
而你，自認是施予者的你，只是目擊者而已。

至於接受施予的你——你們全是領受者——
不要有感恩的負擔，免得讓自己和施予者難以承受。

你不如以施予者的禮物為羽翼，和他一起飛翔；
倘若太過在意你的負債，
就是懷疑給予者的慷慨，
他本是以寬宏的大地為母、以神為父。

Surely he who is worthy to receive his days and his nights is worthy
of all else from you.
And he who has deserved to drink from the ocean of life deserves to
fill his cup from your little stream.

And what desert greater shall there be than that which lies in the
courage and the confidence, nay the charity, of receiving?
And who are you
that men should rend their bosom and unveil their pride,
that you may see their worth naked and their pride unabashed?

See first that you yourself deserve to be a giver,
and an instrument of giving.
For in truth it is life that gives unto life –
while you, who deem yourself a giver, are but a witness.

And you receivers – and you are all receivers – assume no weight of
gratitude, lest you lay a yoke upon yourself and upon him who gives.

Rather rise together with the giver on his gifts as on wings;
For to be overmindful of your debt,
is to doubt his generosity who has the free-hearted earth for mother,
and God for father.

飲食

On Eating & Drinking

讓你的餐桌成為聖壇，
將那些林野間純真無邪的生命，
奉獻給更純真無邪的人心。

And let your board stand an altar on which the pure and
the innocent of forest and plain are sacrificed for
that which is purer and still more innocent in man.

接著，一個老人，一間旅店的老闆說，
和我們說說「飲食」吧。於是他說：

多希望你們能靠大地的芬芳而活，
好像無根植物一樣，有光線即足以維生。
但既然你們為充飢必須殺生，
為解渴必須剝奪初生動物母親的乳汁，
那就讓這成為一種敬拜的儀式吧；
讓你的餐桌成為聖壇，
將那些林野間純真無邪的生命，
奉獻給更純真無邪的人心。

你殺死一頭野獸時，要在心中對牠說：
「殺死你的那個力量也會殺死我；
我的生命也會耗盡。
因為將你送到我手中的法則，
也會將我送到更強而有力的手裡。
你我的血，
不過是滋養天堂之樹的汁液。」

你用牙齒啃咬蘋果時，要在心中對它說：
「你的種子將活在我的身體裡，
你明日的花蕾將在我心中綻放，

Then an old man, a keeper of an inn, said,
"Speak to us of Eating and Drinking." And he said:

Would that you could live on the fragrance of the earth, and like an
air plant be sustained by the light.
But since you must kill to eat,
and rob the newly born of its mother's milk to quench your thirst,
let it then be an act of worship,
And let your board stand an altar on which the pure and the
innocent of forest and plain are sacrificed for that which is purer and
still more innocent in man.

When you kill a beast say to him in your heart:
"By the same power that slays you, I too am slain;
and I too shall be consumed.
For the law that delivered you into my hand shall deliver me into a
mightier hand.
Your blood and my blood is naught but the sap that feeds the tree of
heaven."

And when you crush an apple with your teeth, say to it in your heart:
"Your seeds shall live in my body,
And the buds of your tomorrow shall blossom in my heart,

你的馨香將是我的氣息，
你我將歡欣共度所有的季節。」

秋天，你採收葡萄園中的葡萄，準備釀酒時，
你要在心中說：
「我也是座葡萄園，
我的果實也將被採收釀酒，
我將像新酒一般存放在永恆的容器中。」

冬天，開瓶斟酒時，
在心中為每一杯酒唱首歌吧；
讓每首歌都唱出對秋天、葡萄園和榨酒機的回憶。

And your fragrance shall be my breath,

And together we shall rejoice through all the seasons."

And in the autumn, when you gather the grapes of your vineyards for
the winepress, say in your heart:
"I too am a vineyard,
and my fruit shall be gathered for the winepress,
And like new wine I shall be kept in eternal vessels."

And in winter, when you draw the wine,
let there be in your heart a song for each cup;
And let there be in the song a remembrance for the autumn days, and
for the vineyard, and for the winepress.

工作

On Work

讓自己不斷勞動，才是真正熱愛生命，
經由勞動去愛生命，
就能親近生命最深邃的祕密。

And in keeping yourself with labour you are in truth loving life,
And to love life through labour is to be intimate
with life's inmost secret.

接著，一個農夫說，跟我們說說「工作」吧。
他回答說：

你必須工作，

才跟得上大地的腳步，才能領略大地的靈魂。

因為懶惰會使你成為歲月的陌生人，

會使你脫離生命的隊伍，

那隊伍莊嚴且不卑不亢地邁向無限。

工作的時候，你就是一管蘆笛，

時光的低語透過你變為音樂。

在天地萬物齊聲合鳴之際，

你們有誰甘願當一枝蘆葦，瘖啞而沉默？

你總是聽人說，

工作是詛咒，勞動是不幸。

但是我要對你說，

你在工作的時候，便實現了一部分大地最深遠的夢想，

這個夢在誕生的那一刻，就已經指派給你了。

讓自己不斷勞動，才是真正熱愛生命，

經由勞動去愛生命，

就能親近生命最深邃的祕密。

Then a ploughman said, "Speak to us of Work."
And he answered, saying:

You work that you may keep pace with the earth
and the soul of the earth.
For to be idle is to become a stranger unto the seasons,
and to step out of life's procession,
that marches in majesty and proud submission towards the infinite.

When you work you are a flute through whose heart the whispering
of the hours turns to music.
Which of you would be a reed, dumb and silent,
when all else sings together in unison?

Always you have been told
that work is a curse and labour a misfortune.
But I say to you
that when you work you fulfill a part of earth's furthest dream,
assigned to you when that dream was born,
And in keeping yourself with labour you are in truth loving life,
And to love life through labour
is to be intimate with life's inmost secret.

然而，你若在痛苦中呼喊生命是磨難，
將維繫肉體生存視為寫在你額頭上的詛咒，
那麼我會說，
唯有你額頭上的汗水，才能洗去上面的字跡。

你也曾聽人說，生命真是黑暗，
你在乏累時也會應和那些疲憊的人。
而我說，生命的確黑暗，除非你心懷熱情，
所有熱情都盲目，除非你有知識，
所有知識都無用，除非你有工作，
所有工作都空洞，除非工作中有愛；
懷著愛工作的時候，
就是把自己、他人和神連結在一起。

怎樣才是懷著愛工作呢？
就是用從你內心抽出的絲線織布，
好像你心愛的人即將穿上它。
就是用情感去蓋一間屋子，
好像你心愛的人即將住在裡面。
就是溫柔地播種，歡喜地收割，
好像你心愛的人即將享用那果實。
就是將你的精神注入你創造的一切事物，
並且知道所有受祝福的故人，
都站在你的四周守望。

But if you in your pain call birth an affliction and the support of the flesh a curse written upon your brow,

then I answer that naught but the sweat of your brow shall wash away that which is written.

You have been told also that life is darkness,

and in your weariness you echo what was said by the weary.

And I say that life is indeed darkness save when there is urge,

And all urge is blind save when there is knowledge.

And all knowledge is vain save when there is work,

And all work is empty save when there is love;

And when you work with love you bind yourself to yourself,

and to one another, and to God.

And what is it to work with love?

It is to weave the cloth with threads drawn from your heart,

even as if your beloved were to wear that cloth.

It is to build a house with affection,

even as if your beloved were to dwell in that house.

It is to sow seeds with tenderness and reap the harvest with joy,

even as if your beloved were to eat the fruit.

It is to charge all things you fashion with a breath of your own spirit,

And to know that all the blessed dead

are standing about you and watching.

我常常聽見你們夢囈似地說：

「在大理石上雕刻，而且能在其中瞧見自己靈魂模樣的人，

比耕田種地者更高貴；

能夠抓住彩虹，用它在畫布上畫出人形的人，

要比做鞋者了不起。」

但我不是在睡夢中，而是在正午時分神智清醒地說：

風對巨大橡樹說的話，

不會比對小草說的話更甜蜜；

唯有能用愛將風聲變成動聽歌曲的人，

才是最偉大的人。

工作是愛的具體表現，

如果你不能懷著愛工作，只是邊做邊怨，

那倒不如拋下工作，坐在神殿門口，

接受那些歡喜工作的人的施與。

如果你漠不關心地烤麵包，

就只能烤出讓人半飽的苦麵包。

如果你心懷厭惡地榨葡萄，

你的厭惡就會釀出酒中之毒。

如果你的歌聲有如天使，卻不愛歌唱，

你就像搗住了人們的耳朵，

讓他們聽不見白晝和夜晚的聲音。

Often have I heard you say, as if speaking in sleep,

"He who works in marble, and finds the shape of his own soul in the stone, is nobler than he who ploughs the soil.

And he who seizes the rainbow to lay it on a cloth in the likeness of man, is more than he who makes the sandals for our feet."

But I say, not in sleep but in the over-wakefulness of noontide,

that the wind speaks not more sweetly to the giant oaks than to the least of all the blades of grass;

And he alone is great who turns the voice of the wind into a song made sweeter by his own loving.

Work is love made visible.

And if you cannot work with love but only with distaste,

it is better that you should leave your work and sit at the gate of the temple and take alms of those who work with joy.

For if you bake bread with indifference,

you bake a bitter bread that feeds but half man's hunger.

And if you grudge the crushing of the grapes,

your grudge distills a poison in the wine.

And if you sing though as angels, and love not the singing,

you muffle man's ears to the voices of the day

and the voices of the night.

歡樂與悲傷

On Joy & Sorrow

歡樂的時候，凝視你的內心深處，
你會發現，只有曾經讓你悲傷的事，才會在此刻給你歡樂。
悲傷的時候，再次凝視你的內心深處，
你會發現，其實你是為了曾經帶給你歡樂的事情而哭泣。

When you are joyous, look deep into your heart and you shall find
it is only that which has given you sorrow that is giving you joy.
When you are sorrowful, look again in your heart. and you shall see
that in truth you are weeping for that which has been your delight.

然後，一個婦人說，和我們談談「歡樂」與「悲傷」吧。
他回答：

你的歡樂是未加掩飾的悲傷。

湧出歡笑的那口井，

往往也裝滿了你的淚水。

難道可能有別種情況？

悲傷在你身上鑿刻的痕跡越深，

你能承受的歡樂就越多。

用來盛酒的酒杯，

不就是在陶匠的窯裡燒過嗎？

撫慰你心靈的笛子，

不就是用刀刨空的木頭？

歡樂的時候，

凝視你的內心深處，

你會發現，

只有曾經讓你悲傷的事，才會在此刻給你歡樂。

悲傷的時候，

再次凝視你的內心深處，

你會發現，

其實你是為了曾經帶給你歡樂的事情而哭泣。

T hen a woman said, "Speak to us of Joy and Sorrow."
And he answered:

Your joy is your sorrow unmasked.
And the selfsame well from which your laughter rises was oftentimes
filled with your tears.
And how else can it be?

The deeper that sorrow carves into your being,
the more joy you can contain.
Is not the cup that holds your wine the very cup that was burned in
the potter's oven?
And is not the lute that soothes your spirit,
the very wood that was hollowed with knives?

When you are joyous,
 look deep into your heart
and you shall find
it is only that which has given you sorrow that is giving you joy.
When you are sorrowful,
look again in your heart,
and you shall see
that in truth you are weeping for that which has been your delight.

有些人說：「歡樂比悲傷偉大。」

也有人說：「不，悲傷比較偉大。」

但我要告訴你們，兩者是分不開的。

它們總是一同到來，

當你和其中一者同坐桌前時，

記得，另一個正在你的床上酣睡。

的確，你好像天平一樣，

擺盪在悲傷與歡樂之間。

唯有在空無一念時，你才能靜止平衡。

看守財物的人提起你去秤金量銀的時候，

你的歡樂與悲傷必然也隨之起落吧。

Some of you say, "Joy is greater than sorrow,"

and others say, "Nay, sorrow is the greater."

But I say unto you, they are inseparable.

Together they come,

and when one sits alone with you at your board,

remember that the other is asleep upon your bed.

Verily you are suspended like scales

between your sorrow and your joy.

Only when you are empty are you at standstill and balanced.

When the treasure-keeper lifts you to weigh his gold and his silver,

needs must your joy or your sorrow rise or fall.

第 9 章

房屋

On Houses

再怎麼富麗堂皇的房屋，

也無法守住你的祕密，或是遮掩你的渴念。

因為你的心無邊無際，它住在天空這座大宅裡，

晨霧是它的門，

夜晚的歌聲和靜默是它的窗。

And though of magnificence and splendour,

your house shall not hold your secret nor shelter your longing.

For that which is boundless in you abides in the mansion of the sky,

whose door is the morning mist,

and whose windows are the songs and the silences of night.

然後，一個泥水匠上前說，跟我們講講「房屋」吧。
他回答說：

在城內蓋一棟房屋之前，
先用你的想像在曠野中搭一座涼亭吧。
你在薄暮時分有家可歸，
你心中那個總是遙遠又孤單的流浪者，也應該如此。

你的房屋是你身體的延伸。
它在陽光下成長，在靜夜中沉睡；
它也會做夢。
難道你的房屋不會做夢？
不會夢想離開城市，走向樹林或山巔？

但願我能將你們的房屋全握在手裡，
如同播種般把它們遍撒在森林和草原上。

但願山谷就是你們的街道，
綠徑是你們的巷弄，
你們可以穿過葡萄園尋找彼此，
衣服上沾著泥土的芳香。
然而這些都還不能實現。

Then a mason came forth and said, "Speak to us of Houses".
And he answered and said:

Build of your imaginings a bower in the wilderness ere you build a
house within the city walls.
For even as you have home-comings in your twilight,
so has the wanderer in you, the ever distant and alone.

Your house is your larger body.
It grows in the sun and sleeps in the stillness of the night;
and it is not dreamless.
Does not your house dream?
And dreaming, leave the city for grove or hilltop?

Would that I could gather your houses into my hand,
and like a sower scatter them in forest and meadow.

Would the valleys were your streets,
and the green paths your alleys,
that you might seek one another through vineyards,
and come with the fragrance of the earth in your garments.
But these things are not yet to be.

你們的祖先因為驚懼，所以緊緊挨在一起，
這種恐懼將會持續一段時間。
你們的住屋與田地之間
暫時仍得隔著城牆。

告訴我，歐法里斯的人們，你們的房子裡有些什麼？
你們用緊鎖的門扉守護的是什麼？

你們有平靜嗎？
那能展露你們力量的平靜。
你們有回憶嗎？
回憶就像座橫跨在心靈頂端的閃亮拱門。
你們有美感嗎？
美感能透過木石器物引領心靈直上神聖的山嶽。
告訴我，你們房屋裡有這些嗎？

或者，你們有的只是安逸，以及對安逸的貪欲？
貪欲是個鬼祟的東西，剛進屋裡時還是客人，
然後借住下來，最後成了主人。

是啊，它變成了馴獸師，
拿著鉤子和鞭子，把你更大的欲念變成它的傀儡。

In their fear your forefathers gathered you too near together.

And that fear shall endure a little longer.

A little longer shall your city walls

separate your hearths from your fields.

And tell me, people of Orphalese, what have you in these houses?

And what is it you guard with fastened doors?

Have you peace,

the quiet urge that reveals your power?

Have you remembrances,

the glimmering arches that span the summits of the mind?

Have you beauty, that leads the heart from things fashioned of wood

and stone to the holy mountain?

Tell me, have you these in your houses?

Or have you only comfort, and the lust for comfort,

that stealthy thing that enters the house a guest,

and then becomes a host, and then a master?

Aye, and it becomes a tamer,

and with hook and scourge makes puppets of your larger desires.

它的雙手雖然柔滑如絲，心腸卻硬如鐵石。

它誘你入睡，只為了站在你的床邊，

嘲笑血肉之軀的尊嚴；

它嘲弄你清明的神智，

把它放在鵝絨上，好像易碎的器皿。

的確，貪戀安逸會謀殺靈魂的熱情，

之後獰笑著走過葬禮。

然而你們，曠野的孩子們，歇息時亦不得安歇的人，

你們不會落入陷阱，也不會被馴服。

你們的房屋不是船錨，而是桅杆。

它不是一層蓋住傷口的閃亮薄膜，

而是保護眼睛的眼瞼。

你不可以為了穿過門扉而收起羽翼，

不可以為了避免碰到天花板而低頭，

也不可以為了害怕牆壁坍塌而屏住呼吸；

你不可以住在死人為活人造的墳墓裡。

再怎麼富麗堂皇的房屋，

也無法守住你的祕密，或是遮掩你的渴念。

因為你的心無邊無際，它住在天空這座大宅裡，

晨霧是它的門，

夜晚的歌聲和靜默是它的窗。

Though its hands are silken, its heart is of iron.

It lulls you to sleep only to stand by your bed

and jeer at the dignity of the flesh.

It makes mock of your sound senses,

and lays them in thistledown like fragile vessels.

Verily the lust for comfort murders the passion of the soul,

and then walks grinning in the funeral.

But you, children of space, you restless in rest,

you shall not be trapped nor tamed.

Your house shall be not an anchor but a mast.

It shall not be a glistening film that covers a wound,

but an eyelid that guards the eye.

You shall not fold your wings that you may pass through doors,

nor bend your heads that they strike not against a ceiling,

nor fear to breathe lest walls should crack and fall down.

You shall not dwell in tombs made by the dead for the living.

And though of magnificence and splendour,

your house shall not hold your secret nor shelter your longing.

For that which is boundless in you abides in the mansion of the sky,

whose door is the morning mist,

and whose windows are the songs and the silences of night.

衣服

On Clothes

但願你們能多以皮膚迎向陽光和風，

少依賴衣服。

因為生命的氣息在陽光裡，

生命之手在風中。

Would that you could meet the sun and the wind with

more of your skin and less of your raiment.

For the breath of life is in the sunlight and

the hand of life is in the wind.

　　　　名織工說，跟我們談談衣服吧。

　　　　他回答：

衣服遮蔽了你們許多的美，

卻無法掩蓋醜陋。

雖然你想從衣裝中尋求隱密的自由，

卻也可能從中找到束縛和鎖鏈。

但願你們能多以皮膚迎向陽光和風，

少依賴衣服。

因為生命的氣息在陽光裡，生命之手在風中。

有人說：

「我們穿的衣服是北風織成的。」

我說，是啊，是北風。

然而，羞恥是它的織布機，

柔軟的筋腱是它的絲線。

它做完了工作，就在森林裡歡笑。

不要忘了，端莊是抵擋齷齪眼光的盾牌。

沒有了齷齪小人，

端莊豈不就成為心靈的桎梏？

也不要忘了，大地喜歡撫摸你的赤足，

風也渴望與你的髮絲嬉戲。

And the weaver said, "Speak to us of Clothes".
And he answered:

Your clothes conceal much of your beauty,

yet they hide not the unbeautiful.

And though you seek in garments the freedom of privacy

you may find in them a harness and a chain.

Would that you could meet the sun and the wind with more of your

skin and less of your raiment.

For the breath of life is in the sunlight and the hand of life is in the wind.

Some of you say,

"It is the north wind who has woven the clothes we wear."

And I say, Aye, it was the north wind,

But shame was his loom,

and the softening of the sinews was his thread.

And when his work was done he laughed in the forest.

Forget not that modesty is for a shield against the eye of the unclean.

And when the unclean shall be no more,

what were modesty but a fetter and a fouling of the mind?

And forget not that the earth delights to feel your bare feet and the

winds long to play with your hair.

買賣

On Buying & Selling

你們經由交換大地給予的禮物，
就能享有豐裕，得到滿足。
但交換時，若非憑著愛心和慈悲的正義，
將會使得一些人貪婪，另一些人挨餓。

It is in exchanging the gifts of the earth

that you shall find abundance and be satisfied.

Yet unless the exchange be in love and kindly justice.

it will but lead some to greed and others to hunger.

——個商人說，和我們談談「買賣」吧。

　　他回答道：

大地結出果實給你，

只要懂得如何盛滿你的雙手，你將不致匱乏。

你們經由交換大地給予的禮物，

就能享有豐裕，得到滿足。

但交換時，若非憑著愛心和慈悲的正義，

將會使得一些人貪婪，另一些人挨餓。

來到市場，

你們這些在海上、田裡和葡萄園中辛勞工作的人，

會遇見織工、陶匠和採集香料者——

你們要召請大地之神降臨，

尊崇量秤和物價的計算法。

不要讓空手而來的人參與你們的交易，

因為他們只有滿口空言，

卻想換取你們的勞力。

對這種人，你應當說：

「隨我們下田，

或是和我們兄弟一同出海，撒下你的網；

陸地和海洋也會賜你富足，一如對我們那樣。」

And a merchant said, "Speak to us of Buying and Selling."
And he answered and said:

To you the earth yields her fruit,
and you shall not want if you but know how to fill your hands.
It is in exchanging the gifts of the earth that you shall find abundance
and be satisfied.
Yet unless the exchange be in love and kindly justice,
it will but lead some to greed and others to hunger.

When in the market-place you toilers of the sea and fields and
vineyards meet the weavers and the potters and the gatherers of
spices, –
Invoke then the master spirit of the earth,
to come into your midst and sanctify the scales and the reckoning
that weighs value against value.

And suffer not the barren-handed to take part in your transactions,
who would sell their words for your labour.
To such men you should say:
"Come with us to the field,
or go with our brothers to the sea and cast your net;
For the land and the sea shall be bountiful to you even as to us."

市場上若有歌手、舞者和吹笛人，

你也要買他們與生俱來的才能。

因為他們也是採集果實和乳香的人，

他們帶來的東西雖然如夢似幻，

卻是靈魂的衣裳和食糧。

離開市場之前，

不要讓任何人空手而返。

因為大地之神總要滿足你們最基本的需求，

才能睡得安穩。

And if there come the singers and the dancers and the flute players, –
buy of their gifts also.

For they too are gatherers of fruit and frankincense,

and that which they bring, though fashioned of dreams,

is raiment and food for your soul.

And before you leave the market-place,

see that no one has gone his way with empty hands.

For the master spirit of the earth shall not sleep peacefully upon the

wind till the needs of the least of you are satisfied.

罪與罰

On Crime & Punishment

一片樹葉如果沒有整棵樹的默許，
就不會變黃；
你們所有人的心中如果沒有隱藏惡念，
罪人就不會犯錯。

And as a single leaf turns not yellow
but with the silent knowledge of the whole tree,
So the wrong-doer cannot do wrong
without the hidden will of you all.

然後，城裡一位法官走上前說，
請跟我們講講「罪與罰」吧。
於是他回答說：

當你的心神隨風飄蕩，
你在孤單而毫無防備的情況下，
對別人行了不義之事，就等於是對自己行不義。
為了彌補這個過失，你必須在有福者的門外敲門等候，
但一時之間，將無人理睬你。

你的心中有一個神性自我，
它有如海洋，永遠不會被玷汙。
它也像蒼穹，只幫助有羽翼的鳥獸高飛。
你心中的神性甚至像太陽；
它不知道鼴鼠的地道，
也不去尋找蛇的洞穴。

但是你的心中不只住著神性自我。
你的內心有一部分是人，
還有一大部分並非人，
而是個不成形的侏儒，
他在迷霧中夢遊，尋找自己的覺醒。

T hen one of the judges of the city stood forth and said,
"Speak to us of Crime and Punishment."
And he answered, saying:

It is when your spirit goes wandering upon the wind,

That you, alone and unguarded,

commit a wrong unto others and therefore unto yourself.

And for that wrong committed must you knock and wait a while

unheeded at the gate of the blessed.

Like the ocean is your god-self;

It remains for ever undefiled.

And like the ether it lifts but the winged.

Even like the sun is your god-self;

It knows not the ways of the mole

nor seeks it the holes of the serpent.

But your god-self dwells not alone in your being.

Much in you is still man,

and much in you is not yet man,

But a shapeless pigmy

that walks asleep in the mist searching for its own awakening.

現在我要說的，是你心中的那個人。

因為那個人才懂得罪與罰，

而不是你心中的神性，也不是迷霧中的侏儒。

我常聽你們說起某個犯錯的人，

彷彿他不是你們其中的一分子，

而是闖入你們世界的陌生人。

但是我說，就算是那些聖者賢人，

也無法超越你們人人皆有的至高本質。

同樣的，惡人與弱者，

也不比你們個個都有的卑劣本質更低下。

一片樹葉如果沒有整棵樹的默許，

就不會變黃；

你們所有人的心中如果沒有隱藏惡念，

罪人就不會犯錯。

你們就像一支行進中的隊伍，一起走向自己心中的神性，

你們是道路，也是路上的旅人。

你們之中有人跌倒時，

也是為了提醒後面的人要當心絆腳石；

不過，他也是因為前面的人才會跌倒，

前面的人雖然走得快，腳步穩，

卻沒有搬開絆腳的石頭。

And of the man in you would I now speak.

For it is he and not your god-self nor the pigmy in the mist,

that knows crime and the punishment of crime.

Oftentimes have I heard you speak of one who commits a wrong

as though he were not one of you,

but a stranger unto you and an intruder upon your world.

But I say that even as the holy and the righteous

cannot rise beyond the highest which is in each one of you,

So the wicked and the weak cannot fall lower than the lowest which

is in you also.

And as a single leaf turns not yellow

but with the silent knowledge of the whole tree,

So the wrong-doer cannot do wrong

without the hidden will of you all.

Like a procession you walk together towards your god-self.

You are the way and the wayfarers.

And when one of you falls down he falls for those behind him,

a caution against the stumbling stone.

Aye, and he falls for those ahead of him,

who though faster and surer of foot,

yet removed not the stumbling stone.

雖然以下這些話語會使你的心情無比沉重：
遭殺害的人，對自己慘遭殺害不是毫無責任，
遇搶劫的人，對自己遇到搶劫也不是毫無過失。
正人君子對惡人的惡行並非全然無辜，
清白的好人與罪犯的行為也不是毫無關係。

是的，犯罪者常常是受害人的犧牲品；
獲判死罪的人更常常替無罪者、無過者
背負沉重的負擔。
你們分不清正與邪，
辨不明善與惡；
因為正邪、善惡站在太陽面前，
就如同黑線白線交織在一起。
當黑線斷了，
織工不只要檢查布，
也應該要檢查織布機。

如果你們當中有人要審判不忠的妻子，
也請先秤一秤她丈夫的心，
量一量他的靈魂。
也請想要鞭笞罪犯的人，
先審視受害者的靈魂。

And this also, though the word lie heavy upon your hearts:

The murdered is not unaccountable for his own murder,

And the robbed is not blameless in being robbed.

The righteous is not innocent of the deeds of the wicked,

And the white-handed is not clean in the doings of the felon.

Yea, the guilty is oftentimes the victim of the injured,

And still more often the condemned is the burden bearer

for the guiltless and unblamed.

You cannot separate the just from the unjust

and the good from the wicked;

For they stand together before the face of the sun even as the black

thread and the white are woven together.

And when the black thread breaks,

the weaver shall look into the whole cloth,

and he shall examine the loom also.

If any of you would bring to judgment the unfaithful wife,

Let him also weigh the heart of her husband in scales,

and measure his soul with measurements.

And let him who would lash the offender

look unto the spirit of the offended.

如果你們當中有人要以正義之名懲罰別人，

拿起斧頭要揮向邪惡之樹，

請先讓他看看樹根；

他必將發現善與惡的根、結果實和不結果實的根，

全都在大地靜默的心中纏繞在一起。

而你們這些心存公正的法官啊，

你們如何宣判

身體誠實、內心欺盜的人？

你們如何懲罰

殺害別人軀體，自己的心靈卻飽受凌虐的人？

你們如何起訴

那些欺騙、壓迫他人，

但自己也遭受迫害而憤憤不平的人？

你們又如何懲罰

痛改前非的人？

悔恨不正是你們欣然服膺的法律

所欲伸張的正義嗎？

但你們卻無法將悔恨加在無辜者身上，

也無法將罪人從悔恨中釋放出來。

痛悔總是在夜裡不請而來，

使人清醒，細看自己。

And if any of you would punish in the name of righteousness and lay the axe unto the evil tree,

let him see to its roots;

And verily he will find the roots of the good and the bad, the fruitful and the fruitless, all entwined together in the silent heart of the earth.

And you judges who would be just.

What judgment pronounce you upon him

who though honest in the flesh yet is a thief in spirit?

What penalty lay you upon him

who slays in the flesh yet is himself slain in the spirit?

And how prosecute you him

who in action is a deceiver and an oppressor,

Yet who also is aggrieved and outraged?

And how shall you punish those whose remorse is already greater than their misdeeds?

Is not remorse the justice which is administered by that very law which you would fain serve?

Yet you cannot lay remorse upon the innocent nor lift it from the heart of the guilty.

Unbidden shall it call in the night,

that men may wake and gaze upon themselves.

而你們這些想要了解正義的人哪，
除非是在充足的光線下檢視所有的行為，
否則如何能夠明白正義？

只有那時你才會知道，
站立的和倒下的不過是同一個人，
他就站在侏儒的夜晚和神性的白晝之間的朦朧地帶；
而神殿的房角石，
並不比地基中最低的石頭高。

And you who would understand justice,

how shall you unless you look upon all deeds in the fullness of light?

Only then shall you know that the erect and the fallen are but one
man standing in twilight between the night of his pigmy-self and the
day of his god-self,

And that the corner-stone of the temple is not higher than the lowest
stone in its foundation.

第 13 章

法律

On Laws

你們喜歡制定法律，
卻更喜歡違背它。
好像孩子們在海邊玩耍，
他們一心一意堆起沙堡，
然後又笑著摧毀它。

You delight in laying down laws,
Yet you delight more in breaking them.
Like children playing by the ocean
who build sand-towers with constancy
and then destroy them with laughter.

──個律師接著問，

　　　　但是大師，我們的「法律」又如何呢？

他回答：

你們喜歡制定法律，

卻更喜歡違背它。

好像孩子們在海邊玩耍，

他們一心一意堆起沙堡，

然後又笑著摧毀它。

不過，你堆沙堡的時候，

海洋會把更多的沙子沖上岸；

而你推倒沙堡時，

海洋也和你一起大笑。

的確，大海總是和天真的人一同歡笑。

但是，有些人不把生命看成海洋，

也不把人為的法律看成沙堡，

這些人是怎麼想的呢？

他們認為生命是岩石，

法律是鑿子，

他們用法律這把鑿子雕出自己的模樣。

T hen a lawyer said,
  "But what of our Laws, master?"
And he answered:

You delight in laying down laws,
Yet you delight more in breaking them.
Like children playing by the ocean
who build sand-towers with constancy
and then destroy them with laughter.

But while you build your sand-towers
the ocean brings more sand to the shore,
And when you destroy them
the ocean laughs with you.
Verily the ocean laughs always with the innocent.

But what of those to whom life is not an ocean,
and man-made laws are not sand-towers,
But to whom life is a rock,
and the law a chisel
with which they would carve it in their own likeness?

討厭舞者的瘸子，該怎麼說他呢？

牛愛自己的重軛，卻以為森林裡的鹿是無家可歸的流浪漢，

要怎麼說牠呢？

老蛇蛻不掉自己的皮，卻罵其他的蛇赤身露體，不知羞恥，

又該怎麼說牠呢？

倘若有人早早來到婚宴，

酒足飯飽後疲累地離開，

卻說所有酒宴都違法，

每個賓客皆犯紀，這種人又怎麼說？

對於這些人，我能說什麼呢？

只能說他們雖然站在陽光下，卻是背對著太陽。

他們只看得見自己的影子，

他們的影子就是法律。

對他們來說，太陽不就是個投射影子的東西？

而承認法律，

不就是彎身在地上搜尋自己的影子？

但是，面向太陽行走的你們，

地上的影子哪能攔得住你？

御風而行的你們，

什麼風向標能夠指引你的路？

What of the cripple who hates dancers?

What of the ox who loves his yoke and deems the elk and deer of the

forest stray and vagrant things?

What of the old serpent who cannot shed his skin,

and calls all others naked and shameless?

And of him who comes early to the wedding feast,

and when over-fed and tired goes his way

saying that all feasts are violation

and all feasters law-breakers?

What shall I say of these save that they too stand in the sunlight,

but with their backs to the sun?

They see only their shadows,

and their shadows are their laws.

And what is the sun to them but a caster of shadows?

And what is it to acknowledge the laws but to stoop down and trace

their shadows upon the earth?

But you who walk facing the sun,

what images drawn on the earth can hold you?

You who travel with the wind,

what weather vane shall direct your course?

你若是掙脫自己的束縛，卻不打破別人的牢門，

什麼樣的法律能夠約束你？

你若是跳舞，卻不絆倒在別人的鐵鏈上，

有什麼法律能令你害怕？

你若是撕裂衣服，卻不丟在他人的小徑上，

有誰可以帶你上法庭？

歐法里斯的人們啊，

你們可以蒙住鼓聲，

也可以調鬆琴弦，

但是誰能命令雲雀噤聲不唱？

What man's law shall bind you if you break your yoke but upon no man's prison door?

What laws shall you fear if you dance but stumble against no man's iron chains?

And who is he that shall bring you to judgment if you tear off your garment yet leave it in no man's path?

People of Orphalese,

you can muffle the drum,

and you can loosen the strings of the lyre,

but who shall command the skylark not to sing?

第14章

自由

On Freedom

而我的心在淌血，

因為唯有你覺悟到追尋自由的欲望成為你的束縛，

唯有你不再將自由視為目標和成就時，

你才能夠真正地自由。

And my heart bled within me;

for you can only be free when even the desire of seeking freedom

becomes a harness to you,

and when you cease to speak of freedom as a goal and a fulfillment.

個演說家說，跟我們講講「自由」吧。

　　　他回答說：

我看見你們在城門口和火爐邊，

頂禮膜拜自己的自由，

猶如奴隸卑微地屈膝於暴君面前，讚揚他，

雖然他殺害了奴隸。

是啊，在神殿的樹叢中，在城堡的陰影裡，

我見過你們當中最自由的人，

把自由像牛軛與手銬似地，套在自己身上。

而我的心在淌血，

因為唯有你覺悟到追尋自由的欲望成為你的束縛，

唯有你不再將自由視為目標和成就時，

你才能夠真正地自由。

的確，你的白天不免有牽掛，

你的夜晚仍有匱乏和憂傷，

當這些事情籠緊你的生活，

你卻能坦然超脫，不受羈絆，

那時你才是真正地自由。

And an orator said, Speak to us of Freedom.
And he answered:

At the city gate and by your fireside I have seen you prostrate yourself and worship your own freedom,
Even as slaves humble themselves before a tyrant and praise him though he slays them.

Aye, in the grove of the temple and in the shadow of the citadel
I have seen the freest among you
wear their freedom as a yoke and a handcuff.

And my heart bled within me;
for you can only be free when even the desire of seeking freedom becomes a harness to you,
and when you cease to speak of freedom as a goal and a fulfillment.

You shall be free indeed when your days are not without a care
nor your nights without a want and a grief,
But rather when these things girdle your life
and yet you rise above them naked and unbound.

你的了悟才漸露曙光，

卻已被繫上正午的鎖鏈，

除非你能夠掙脫它們，否則你如何超越白天與黑夜？

其實你所說的自由，是這些鎖鏈中最牢固的一條，

只是它的鏈環在陽光下閃閃發亮，眩惑了你的雙眼。

你為了獲取自由而拋棄的東西，

不就是自我的碎片嗎？

你要廢除的那條不公正的法律，

也是你當初親手寫在自己額頭上的。

哪怕是焚燒法律書籍，或傾倒海水來沖洗法官的額頭，

你仍無法抹去不公的法律。

如果你想推翻一個暴君，

必先確知他建立在你心裡的王座已遭摧毀。

暴君如何能宰制自由且自豪的人民？

不就是因為人民的自由中隱藏了專橫，

驕傲中充滿了羞恥？

如果你想拋開顧慮，

那些顧慮也是你自己選的，不是別人給的。

如果你想驅除恐懼，

恐懼就坐落在你心中，而不是在你懼怕的人手裡。

And how shall you rise beyond your days and nights unless you break
the chains which you at the dawn of your understanding have
fastened around your noon hour?
In truth that which you call freedom is the strongest of these chains,
though its links glitter in the sun and dazzle your eyes.

And what is it but fragments of your own self you would discard that
you may become free?
If it is an unjust law you would abolish, that law was written with
your own hand upon your own forehead.
You cannot erase it by burning your law books nor by washing the
foreheads of your judges, though you pour the sea upon them.

And if it is a despot you would dethrone,
see first that his throne erected within you is destroyed.
For how can a tyrant rule the free and the proud,
but for a tyranny in their own freedom
and a shame in their own pride?

And if it is a care you would cast off,
that care has been chosen by you rather than imposed upon you.
And if it is a fear you would dispel,
the seat of that fear is in your heart and not in the hand of the feared.

的確，存在於你生命中的一切，

你渴望的和害怕的，

你厭惡的和珍愛的，

你追求的和逃離的，

這些事物總是游移不定，若即若離。

這些東西在你心中不斷盤旋，

有如光和影成雙成對，相依相從。

一旦影子消失不見，

徘徊不去的光線便成為另一道光的影子。

同樣的，當你的自由掙脫了它的腳鐐，

它便成為更大自由的枷鎖。

Verily all things move within your being in constant half embrace,

the desired and the dreaded,

the repugnant and the cherished,

the pursued and that which you would escape.

These things move within you

as lights and shadows in pairs that cling.

And when the shadow fades and is no more,

the light that lingers becomes a shadow to another light.

And thus your freedom when it loses its fetters becomes itself the

fetter of a greater freedom.

第 15 章

理智與情感

On Reason & Passion

理智和情感

是你的靈魂航行時的船舵與風帆。

倘若風帆或船舵其中一個損壞，

你便只能在海上翻騰漂流，

或是滯留在汪洋大海中。

Your reason and your passion

are the rudder and he sails of your seafaring soul.

If either your sails or your rudder be broken,

you can but toss and drift,

or else be held at a standstill in mid-seas.

這時，女祭司又開口說道，
跟我們說說「理智與情感」吧。

他回答：

你的靈魂是個戰場，
你的理智和判斷、你的情感和欲念
經常在其中交戰。

我多希望自己是你靈魂的和事佬，
將你性情中的衝突與對立，
化為一致和悅耳的旋律。
但是我如何能做得到？
除非你自己也是和事佬；
不，不僅如此，你必須熱愛你性情中所有的特質。

理智和情感
是你的靈魂航行時的船舵與風帆。
倘若風帆或船舵其中一個損壞，
你便只能在海上翻騰漂流，
或是滯留在汪洋大海中。

因為理智單獨主宰的時候，它是一種局限的力量；
而情感若不多加留意，就會變成焚毀自己的火焰。

And the priestess spoke again and said:
"Speak to us of Reason and Passion."
And he answered, saying:

Your soul is oftentimes a battlefield,
upon which your reason and your judgment wage war against your
passion and your appetite.

Would that I could be the peacemaker in your soul,
that I might turn the discord and the rivalry of your elements into
oneness and melody.
But how shall I,
unless you yourselves be also the peacemakers,
nay, the lovers of all your elements?

Your reason and your passion are the rudder and the sails of your
seafaring soul.
If either your sails or your rudder be broken,
you can but toss and drift,
or else be held at a standstill in mid-seas.

For reason, ruling alone, is a force confining;
and passion, unattended, is a flame that burns to its own destruction.

因此，就讓你的靈魂將理智提升到情感的高度，
使理智高歌；
也讓靈魂用理智引導你的情感，
使你的情感能夠每日重生，
如同從自己的灰燼中復活的鳳凰。

我希望你把判斷和欲念
設想為家中兩位心愛的貴客。
你當然不會只禮遇一人，而怠慢另一人，
因為對任何一個客人偏心，就會失去兩人的愛與信賴。

當你坐在山巒之間
涼爽的白楊樹蔭底下，
享受遠方田野與草原的寧靜祥和時——
請讓你的心默默地說：「神在理智中安歇。」
當暴風雨來臨，
狂風撼動森林，
雷鳴與閃電宣示天空的威嚴時，
請讓你的心敬畏地說：「神在情感中行事。」

既然你是神的世界中的一縷氣息，
是神的森林中的一片樹葉，
你也應該在理智中安歇，在情感中行事。

Therefore let your soul exalt your reason to the height of passion,

that it may sing;

And let it direct your passion with reason,

that your passion may live through its own daily resurrection,

and like the phoenix rise above its own ashes.

I would have you consider your judgment and your appetite even as

you would two loved guests in your house.

Surely you would not honour one guest above the other;

for he who is more mindful of one loses the love and the faith of both.

Among the hills,

when you sit in the cool shade of the white poplars,

sharing the peace and serenity of distant fields and meadows –

then let your heart say in silence, "God rests in reason."

And when the storm comes,

and the mighty wind shakes the forest,

and thunder and lightning proclaim the majesty of the sky, –

then let your heart say in awe, "God moves in passion."

And since you are a breath in God's sphere,

and a leaf in God's forest,

you too should rest in reason and move in passion.

痛苦

On Pain

如果你能讓心靈驚嘆於
生命中天天發生的奇蹟，
你的痛苦將會和快樂一樣奇妙。

And could you keep your heart in wonder at
the daily miracles of your life,
your pain would not seem less wondrous than your joy:

個婦人說，請告訴我們關於「痛苦」的事。
　　　於是他說：

你感覺痛苦是因為你衝破了裹住理解力的那層外殼。

如同果核必須迸裂，

核心才能暴露在陽光下，你也必須了解痛苦。

如果你能讓心靈驚嘆於

生命中天天發生的奇蹟，

你的痛苦將會和快樂一樣奇妙。

你也將能接納心中的季節變化，

一如你向來接受走過你田地的四季變換，

你將能平靜地目送你悲傷的冬日。

你的痛苦多半是自尋煩惱，

那是你內心的醫生

為治癒你的病痛所下的苦藥。

所以，要相信你的醫生，

沉默且平靜地喝下這帖藥吧：

他雖然出手既重又猛，

卻是由看不見的神那雙溫柔之手引導；

他帶來的杯子雖然燙嘴，

卻是神這位陶匠，用祂神聖的淚水滴溼的泥土燒成。

And a woman spoke, saying, "Tell us of Pain."
And he said:

Your pain is the breaking of the shell that encloses your understanding.
Even as the stone of the fruit must break,
that its heart may stand in the sun, so must you know pain.

And could you keep your heart in wonder at
the daily miracles of your life,
your pain would not seem less wondrous than your joy;
And you would accept the seasons of your heart, even as you have
always accepted the seasons that pass over your fields.
And you would watch with serenity through the winters of your grief.

Much of your pain is self-chosen.
It is the bitter potion
by which the physician within you heals your sick self.
Therefore trust the physician,
and drink his remedy in silence and tranquillity:
For his hand, though heavy and hard,
is guided by the tender hand of the Unseen,
And the cup he brings, though it burn your lips, has been fashioned
of the clay which the Potter has moistened with His own sacred tears.

第 17 章

自知

On Self-Knowledge

靈魂漫步於所有的道路上，
它不會沿著直線前進，也不會像蘆葦一樣筆直成長。
靈魂會綻放，好像一朵擁有數不清花瓣的蓮花。

For the soul walks upon all paths.

The soul walks not upon a line, neither does it grow like a reed.

The soul unfolds itself. like a lotus of countless petals.

個男人說，和我們談談「自知」吧。

　　　於是他回答：

你的心在靜默中領悟白晝與黑夜的祕密，

但你的耳朵渴望聽見心中知識的聲音。

你想將向來了然於心的事物

化為言語，

你想用手指觸碰

夢裡赤裸的身體。

你確實應該這麼做，

你靈魂中的暗泉必須湧出，

一路潺潺流向大海；

隱藏在你無盡深處的寶藏，

也將展現在你眼前。

但請別秤量那未知寶藏的重量，

也不要用測桿或量繩

探測你知識的深度，

因為自我是大海，

無邊無際，不可量測。

And a man said, "Speak to us of Self-Knowledge."
And he answered, saying:

Your hearts know in silence the secrets of the days and the nights.
But your ears thirst for the sound of your heart's knowledge.

You would know in words
that which you have always known in thought.
You would touch with your fingers
the naked body of your dreams.

And it is well you should.
The hidden well-spring of your soul must needs rise and run
murmuring to the sea;
And the treasure of your infinite depths
would be revealed to your eyes.

But let there be no scales to weigh your unknown treasure;
And seek not the depths of your knowledge
with staff or sounding line.
For self is a sea
boundless and measureless.

別說，「我已找到真理。」

應該說，「我找到一個真理。」

別說，「我已找到靈魂的道路。」

應該說，「我遇見和我同路的靈魂。」

因為靈魂漫步於所有的道路上，

它不會沿著直線前進，也不會像蘆葦一樣筆直成長。

靈魂會綻放，好像一朵擁有數不清花瓣的蓮花。

Say not, "I have found the truth,"

but rather, "I have found a truth."

Say not, "I have found the path of the soul."

Say rather, "I have met the soul walking upon my path."

For the soul walks upon all paths.

The soul walks not upon a line, neither does it grow like a reed.

The soul unfolds itself, like a lotus of countless petals.

教育

On Teaching

老師漫步在神殿的暗影中，

走在門徒之間，

他們奉獻的不是智慧，而是信念與愛心。

The teacher who walks in the shadow of the temple.

among his followers.

gives not of his wisdom but rather of his faith and his lovingness.

然後，一位教師說，跟我們說說「教育」吧。

然他回答：

任何人能夠給你的啟發，

其實都已經在你知識的曙光中半睡半醒。

老師漫步在神殿的暗影中，

走在門徒之間，

他們奉獻的不是智慧，而是信念與愛心。

若他確實睿智，就不會吩咐你進入他的智慧之屋，

而是引導你跨越自己心靈的門檻。

天文學家或許可以與你暢談他對太空的了解，

卻無法把他的理解給你；

音樂家或許可以對你唱出盈滿天地之間的韻律，

卻無法給你掌握節奏的耳朵，

或是應和韻律的歌喉；

精通數字科學的人或許可以告訴你計算和度量的方法，

卻無法帶領你到達彼方。

因為一個人不能把想像力的翅膀借給別人，

就像在神的心中，你們是各自獨立的，

因此，你們也必須獨自認識神和地球。

T hen said a teacher, "Speak to us of Teaching."
And he said:

No man can reveal to you aught but that which already lies half
asleep in the dawning of your knowledge.
The teacher who walks in the shadow of the temple,
among his followers,
gives not of his wisdom but rather of his faith and his lovingness.
If he is indeed wise he does not bid you enter the house of his
wisdom, but rather leads you to the threshold of your own mind.

The astronomer may speak to you of his understanding of space,
but he cannot give you his understanding.
The musician may sing to you of the rhythm which is in all space,
but he cannot give you the ear which arrests the rhythm nor the
voice that echoes it.
And he who is versed in the science of numbers can tell of the regions
of weight and measure, but he cannot conduct you thither.
For the vision of one man lends not its wings to another man.

And even as each one of you stands alone in God's knowledge,
so must each one of you be alone in his knowledge of God and in his
understanding of the earth.

友誼

On Friendship

除了增加心靈的深度之外，
友誼不應有其他目的，
因為絕不揭露自我的愛，並不是真愛，
而是向前撒出的網，
網到的只是無用之物。

And let there be no purpose in friendship
save the deepening of the spirit.
For love that seeks aught but the disclosure of its own mystery
is not love but a net cast forth:
and only the unprofitable is caught.

一個青年說，跟我們說說「友誼」吧。

　　他回答道：

你的朋友可以回應你的需求。

他是你的田地，你用愛播種，以感恩收割；

他也是你的餐桌和爐火，

因為你會在飢餓時到他身邊，

並在他那裡尋求平靜。

朋友對你吐露心事時，不要害怕說出心中的「不」，

也不要吝於說「是」。

他沉默的時候，你的心也不要停止聆聽他的心聲，

因為友情不需要言語，

一切思想，一切欲念，一切期望，

都在無言的歡樂中孕育和分享。

當你和朋友分開時，不要悲傷；

因為他不在的時候，

他那些你最愛的優點將會更清晰，

就像對登山的人而言，在平地看山更清楚。

除了增加心靈的深度之外，

友誼不應有其他目的，

A nd a youth said, "Speak to us of Friendship."
And he answered, saying:

Your friend is your needs answered.

He is your field which you sow with love and reap with thanksgiving.

And he is your board and your fireside.

For you come to him with your hunger,

and you seek him for peace.

When your friend speaks his mind you fear not the "nay" in your

own mind, nor do you withhold the "aye."

And when he is silent your heart ceases not to listen to his heart;

For without words, in friendship,

all thoughts, all desires, all expectations are born and shared,

with joy that is unclaimed.

When you part from your friend, you grieve not;

For that which you love most in him

may be clearer in his absence,

as the mountain to the climber is clearer from the plain.

And let there be no purpose in friendship

save the deepening of the spirit.

因為絕不揭露自我的愛，並不是真愛，

而是向前撒出的網，

網到的只是無用之物。

把你最好的留給你的朋友，

如果他定要知道你的低潮，

也要讓他曉得你潮汐的高漲。

倘若找他只為打發時間，哪算什麼朋友？

你應該找他一同體驗生命。

因為朋友應滿足你的需要，

而不是填補你的空虛。

就讓歡笑和共享的快樂，

充滿甜美的友誼，

因為唯有在如朝露的小事中，

你的心才找到煥然一新的清晨。

For love that seeks aught but the disclosure of its own mystery is not
love but a net cast forth:
and only the unprofitable is caught.

And let your best be for your friend.
If he must know the ebb of your tide,
let him know its flood also.

For what is your friend that you should seek him with hours to kill?
Seek him always with hours to live.
For it is his to fill your need,
but not your emptiness.
And in the sweetness of friendship let there be laughter,
and sharing of pleasures.
For in the dew of little things
the heart finds its morning and is refreshed.

第 20 章

說話

On Talking

你的思想無法為你帶來平靜時，你就會說話；
你無法安居於孤獨的心境時，你就會訴諸脣舌，
使得聲音成為一種娛樂和消遣。

You talk when you cease to be at peace with your thoughts:
And when you can no longer dwell in the solitude of your heart
you live in your lips, and sound is a diversion and a pastime.

之後，一名學者說，和我們談談「說話」吧。
他回答：

你的思想無法為你帶來平靜時，你就會說話；
你無法安居於孤獨的心境時，你就會訴諸脣舌，
使得聲音成為一種娛樂和消遣。
於是，在你大部分的言談中，
思想泰半已被扼殺，
因為思想是空中的飛鳥，
牠在言語的樊籠裡或許可以展翅，卻無法高飛。

你們當中有些人害怕孤單，
所以喜歡與多話的人為伍。
獨處的孤寂暴露了這些人赤裸的自我，
因此他們才要逃避。

有些人說話，
既無知又無遠見，
無法闡明自己不明白的真理。
有些人對真理了然於心，
卻不用言語說出來。
在這些人的胸臆間，心靈安住在有節奏的寂靜裡。

A nd then a scholar said, "Speak of Talking."
And he answered, saying:

You talk when you cease to be at peace with your thoughts;

And when you can no longer dwell in the solitude of your heart you

live in your lips, and sound is a diversion and a pastime.

And in much of your talking,

thinking is half murdered.

For thought is a bird of space,

that in a cage of words may indeed unfold its wings but cannot fly.

There are those among you who seek the talkative through fear of

being alone.

The silence of aloneness reveals to their eyes their naked selves

and they would escape.

And there are those who talk,

and without knowledge or forethought reveal a truth which they

themselves do not understand.

And there are those who have the truth within them,

but they tell it not in words.

In the bosom of such as these the spirit dwells in rhythmic silence.

你在路上或市場遇到朋友的時候，

讓你的心靈牽動你的脣，引導你的舌。

將你心裡的聲音，說進他心中的耳朵；

因為你心靈的真理，會留在他的靈魂中，

一如美酒的滋味，會留在記憶中，

雖然酒的色澤已為人遺忘，酒樽也不復存在。

When you meet your friend on the roadside or in the market-place,

let the spirit in you move your lips and direct your tongue.

Let the voice within your voice speak to the ear of his ear;

For his soul will keep the truth of your heart

as the taste of the wine is remembered.

When the colour is forgotten and the vessel is no more.

時間

On Time

時間豈不像愛一樣，
既分不開也無所謂快慢？
如果你心中非要用季節量測時間，
那麼就讓每個季節之間相互蘊含，
也讓今天以回憶擁抱過去，
用渴望迎向未來。

And is not time even as love is,
undivided and paceless ?
But if in your thought you must measure time into seasons,
let each season encircle all the other seasons.
And let today embrace the past with remembrance
and the future with longing.

　　　　位天文學家說，大師，「時間」又是怎麼回事呢？

　　　　他回答說：

你想度量的是無窮無盡、不可量測的時間。

你想依據時辰和季節調整你的行動，

甚至導引心靈的走向。

你想把時間看作一條溪流，

而你坐在岸邊，看著溪水流動。

但你心中的永恆明白生命是無窮無盡的，

也知道昨天不過是今天的回憶，

明天則是今天的夢想。

而你體內所歌唱與沉思的，

仍存在於宇宙在太初時刻灑落的繁星之間。

你們當中有誰感覺不到

自己愛的力量是無窮無盡的呢？

有誰感覺不到愛雖然無窮無盡，

卻縈繞在生命的中心，

不會在愛的念頭中游移，

也不會在愛的行動中流轉？

A nd an astronomer said, "Master, what of Time?"
And he answered:

You would measure time the measureless and the immeasurable.
You would adjust your conduct and even direct the course of your
spirit according to hours and seasons.
Of time you would make a stream upon whose bank you would sit
and watch its flowing.

Yet the timeless in you is aware of life's timelessness,
And knows that yesterday is but today's memory
and tomorrow is today's dream.
And that which sings and contemplates in you is still dwelling within
the bounds of that first moment which scattered the stars into space.

Who among you does not feel that
his power to love is boundless?
And yet who does not feel that very love, though boundless,
encompassed within the centre of his being,
and moving not from love thought to love thought,
nor from love deeds to other love deeds?

時間豈不像愛一樣，

既分不開也無所謂快慢？

如果你心中非要用季節量測時間，

那麼就讓每個季節之間相互蘊含，

也讓今天以回憶擁抱過去，

用渴望迎向未來。

And is not time even as love is,

undivided and paceless?

But if in your thought you must measure time into seasons,

let each season encircle all the other seasons,

And let today embrace the past with remembrance and the future

with longing.

第22章

善與惡

On Good & Evil

我可以訴說你們心中的善，卻不能訴說惡。
因為惡不就是善飽受自身飢渴折磨之後的結果嗎？

Of the good in you I can speak, but not of the evil.
For what is evil but good tortured by its own hunger and thirst?

城裡一位長者說，請跟我們講講「善與惡」吧。
他回答：

我可以訴說你們心中的善，卻不能訴說惡。
因為惡不就是善飽受自身飢渴折磨之後的結果嗎？
的確，善在飢餓時，會到漆黑的洞穴裡尋找食物；
善在口渴時，甚至不得不啜飲死水。

你和自己合而為一時，你是善良的，
你和自己表裡不一時，也並不邪惡，
因為分裂的家不是賊窩，
只是個分裂的家罷了。
一艘無舵的船可能漫無目的漂流在危險的島嶼間，
但它不會沉入海底。

你努力奉獻自己的時候，你是善良的，
但你為自己求取好處時，也並不邪惡，
因為你為自己追求利益時，
不過就像是緊緊攀附泥土、在她胸脯吸吮乳汁的樹根。
果實當然不能對樹根說：
「你要像我一樣成熟又飽滿，而且總是樂於獻出你的豐饒。」
因為對果實來說，「奉獻」是一種需要，
正如對樹根而言，「接受」是一種需要。

And one of the elders of the city said, "Speak to us of Good and Evil." And he answered:

Of the good in you I can speak, but not of the evil.

For what is evil but good tortured by its own hunger and thirst?

Verily when good is hungry it seeks food even in dark caves,

and when it thirsts it drinks even of dead waters.

You are good when you are one with yourself.

Yet when you are not one with yourself you are not evil.

For a divided house is not a den of thieves;

it is only a divided house.

And a ship without rudder may wander aimlessly among perilous

isles yet sink not to the bottom.

You are good when you strive to give of yourself.

Yet you are not evil when you seek gain for yourself.

For when you strive for gain you are but a root that clings to the

earth and sucks at her breast.

Surely the fruit cannot say to the root,

"Be like me, ripe and full and ever giving of your abundance."

For to the fruit giving is a need,

as receiving is a need to the root.

當你說出完全清醒的言詞時，你是善良的，

但即使你睡著了，

口舌無度、發出囈語時，也並不邪惡。

因為言詞即使結巴，也能鞏固軟弱的舌頭。

你以堅定果敢的步伐邁向目標時，你是善良的，

但你走得一瘸一拐時，也並不邪惡。

因為就算是跛行之人，也並未倒退。

但是，強壯且敏捷的你啊，

可別跛腳走在瘸子前面，還以為這是善意。

你的善行不計其數，

但你不行善時未必就是惡，

你只是閒散和怠惰。

可惜呀，雄鹿教不會烏龜快跑。

你的善在於渴望壯大的自我，

你們心裡都有這種渴望。

但是在你們一些人的心裡，這種渴望是一股激流，

挾帶山坡的祕密和森林的歌曲，滔滔衝向大海。

而另一些人的渴望，則有如一條平靜無波的小溪，

迷失在曲折蜿蜒的河道中，流連徘徊，緩緩流到海岸。

You are good when you are fully awake in your speech.

Yet you are not evil when you sleep while your tongue staggers without purpose.

And even stumbling speech may strengthen a weak tongue.

You are good when you walk to your goal firmly and with bold steps.

Yet you are not evil when you go thither limping.

Even those who limp go not backward.

But you who are strong and swift,

see that you do not limp before the lame, deeming it kindness.

You are good in countless ways,

and you are not evil when you are not good,

You are only loitering and sluggard.

Pity that the stags cannot teach swiftness to the turtles.

In your longing for your giant self lies your goodness:

and that longing is in all of you.

But in some of you that longing is a torrent rushing with might to the sea, carrying the secrets of the hillsides and the songs of the forest.

And in others it is a flat stream that loses itself in angles and bends and lingers before it reaches the shore.

但不要讓多欲的人對寡欲的人說：

「為什麼你如此緩慢，又總是停下不走？」

因為真正善良的人不會問無衣可穿的人：

「你的衣服呢？」

也不會問無家可歸的人：

「你的房子出了什麼事？」

But let not him who longs much say to him who longs little,

"Wherefore are you slow and halting?"

For the truly good ask not the naked,

"Where is your garment?"

nor the houseless,

"What has befallen your house?"

第 23 章

祈禱

On Prayer

你在愁苦和匱乏時祈禱，
但願你也在豐饒富足的日子
和充滿喜樂時祈禱。

You pray in your distress and in your need:
would that you might pray also in the fullness of your joy
and in your days of abundance.

之後，一個女祭司說，跟我們說說「祈禱」吧。
他回答說：

你在愁苦和匱乏時祈禱，

但願你也在豐饒富足的日子

和充滿喜樂時祈禱。

祈禱不就是把自己擴及到靈動的天地宇宙之間嗎？

倘若向天空傾吐你的陰鬱可以給你安慰，

那麼向天空傾訴心中的曙光也可以使你快樂。

倘若你的靈魂召喚你祈禱，

你卻只能哭泣，

她就應該一再鼓舞你，直到你破涕為笑。

當你祈禱時，你將凌空而起，

和其他同在祈禱的人相逢；

在祈禱的時刻之外，你不可能遇見他們。

因此，且讓你前去拜望那無形的神殿吧，

只為了與狂喜和甜蜜的心靈相契，不為其它。

如果你進入這座神殿，只是為了祈求，

你將一無所獲。

如果你進入神殿，是為了貶抑自己，

神不會抬舉你。

T hen a priestess said, "Speak to us of Prayer."
And he answered, saying:

You pray in your distress and in your need;

would that you might pray also in the fullness of your joy

and in your days of abundance.

For what is prayer but the expansion of yourself into the living ether?

And if it is for your comfort to pour your darkness into space,

it is also for your delight to pour forth the dawning of your heart.

And if you cannot but weep when your soul summons you to prayer,

she should spur you again and yet again, though weeping,

until you shall come laughing.

When you pray you rise to meet in the air those who are praying at
that very hour,

and whom save in prayer you may not meet.

Therefore let your visit to that temple invisible be for naught but
ecstasy and sweet communion.

For if you should enter the temple for no other purpose than asking
you shall not receive:

And if you should enter into it to humble yourself
you shall not be lifted:

如果你進入神殿，是為了他人祈福，

神不會聽見你。

你們只要進入無形的神殿，這就已經足夠。

我無法教你禱告詞該怎麼說，

神不會聽你的言語，

除非祂本人經由你的嘴說話。

我也無法教你

海洋、森林和群山的祝禱，

但是你們這些生於群山、森林和海洋的人，

可以在心中找到它們的禱詞。

只要你們願意在靜謐的夜裡傾聽，

就會聽見它們默默地說著：

「我們的神啊，祢是我們長了翅膀的自我，

祢的意願就是我們的意願，

祢的欲念就是我們的欲念。

我們的心受到祢的激勵，

將我們那屬於祢的夜晚變為白晝，這白晝也同樣屬於祢。

我們不能向祢祈求什麼，

因為我們的需求尚未生出之前，祢就已經知道。

祢就是我們的需求；

祢把自己獻給我們，也把一切賜給我們。」

Or even if you should enter into it to beg for the good of others
you shall not be heard.
It is enough that you enter the temple invisible.

I cannot teach you how to pray in words.
God listens not to your words save when He Himself utters them
through your lips.
And I cannot teach you
the prayer of the seas and the forests and the mountains.
But you who are born of the mountains and the forests and the seas
can find their prayer in your heart,
And if you but listen in the stillness of the night you shall hear them
saying in silence:
"Our God, who art our winged self,
it is thy will in us that willeth.
"It is thy desire in us that desireth.
"It is thy urge in us that would turn our nights, which are thine,
into days which are thine also.
"We cannot ask thee for aught,
for thou knowest our needs before they are born in us:
"Thou art our need;
and in giving us more of thyself thou givest us all."

第 24 章

快樂

On Pleasure

是啊，沒錯，
快樂是一首自由之歌，
我樂於讓你全心全意去唱這首歌，
但我不許你在歌唱中迷失自己。

Aye, in very truth,

pleasure is a freedom-song.

And I fain would have you sing it with fullness of heart:

yet I would not have you lose your hearts in the singing.

接著，有個每年進城一次的隱士走上前說，
和我們講一講「快樂」吧。

他回答道：

快樂是一首自由之歌，

但它不是自由。

它是你欲望綻放的花朵，

但不是欲望結出的果實。

它是深谷對高山的呼喊，

但它既非深谷也不是高山。

它是展開雙翼的籠中鳥，

但不是被局限的空間。

是啊，沒錯，

快樂是一首自由之歌，

我樂於讓你全心全意去唱這首歌，

但我不許你在歌唱中迷失自己。

你們當中有些年輕人始終在尋求快樂，彷彿那是一切，

因而受到批評和指責。

我不會批評他們，也不會指責他們，

我要讓他們去追尋，

因為他們必將找到快樂，

而且不只是快樂；

T hen a hermit, who visited the city once a year, came forth and said, "Speak to us of Pleasure."

And he answered, saying:

Pleasure is a freedom-song,

But it is not freedom.

It is the blossoming of your desires,

But it is not their fruit.

It is a depth calling unto a height,

But it is not the deep nor the high.

It is the caged taking wing,

But it is not space encompassed.

Aye, in very truth,

pleasure is a freedom-song.

And I fain would have you sing it with fullness of heart;

yet I would not have you lose your hearts in the singing.

Some of your youth seek pleasure as if it were all,

and they are judged and rebuked.

I would not judge nor rebuke them.

I would have them seek.

For they shall find pleasure,

but not her alone;

快樂有七個姊妹，

其中最平庸的也比快樂還要美麗。

你是否聽過有人想挖出地下的樹根，

卻發現了寶藏？

你們當中有些老人家回憶快樂時心懷悔恨，

好像那是酒醉時犯下的過錯。

但悔恨只是蒙蔽心靈的陰影，而不是責罰。

他們應該以感恩之情回憶快樂，

就像憶起夏季的豐收。

不過，倘若悔恨能安慰他們，那就讓他們得到安慰吧。

你們當中還有一些人，

既不是尋求快樂的年輕人，也不是追憶快樂的老人家；

他們因為害怕尋求與回憶，乾脆逃避所有的快樂，

唯恐忽視或冒犯了性靈。

但即使是這樣，他們的逃避之中仍然有快樂。

他們也發現了寶藏，

雖然他們挖掘樹根的手在顫抖。

但是，告訴我，有誰能夠冒犯性靈？

夜鷹能否冒犯夜晚的靜謐？

螢火蟲能否冒犯星星？

Seven are her sisters,

and the least of them is more beautiful than pleasure.

Have you not heard of the man who was digging in the earth for

roots and found a treasure?

And some of your elders remember pleasures with regret like wrongs

committed in drunkenness.

But regret is the beclouding of the mind and not its chastisement.

They should remember their pleasures with gratitude,

as they would the harvest of a summer.

Yet if it comforts them to regret, let them be comforted.

And there are among you those who are neither young to seek nor

old to remember;

And in their fear of seeking and remembering they shun all pleasures,

lest they neglect the spirit or offend against it.

But even in their foregoing is their pleasure.

And thus they too find a treasure though they dig for roots with

quivering hands.

But tell me, who is he that can offend the spirit?

Shall the nightingale offend the stillness of the night,

or the firefly the stars?

你的火焰或煙霧豈會成為風的負擔？

你以為性靈是一池靜水，一根長竿就能攪亂它？

壓抑快樂不過是

將欲念積存在你的內心深處，

誰知道今天看似遺忘的東西，不會等待在明天出現？

就連你的身體也懂得它天生的權力與理所當然的需要，

不會受到瞞騙。

你的身體是你靈魂的豎琴，

要用它奏出美妙的音樂，或是雜亂的噪音，全由你決定。

此刻，你在心中自問：

「我們如何分辨好的快樂和不好的快樂呢？」

走一趟你的田地和花園，你就會知道，

採集花蜜是蜜蜂的快樂，

但花朵分泌花蜜給蜜蜂採集，也是花朵的快樂；

因為對蜜蜂來說，花朵是生命的泉源，

而對花朵來說，蜜蜂是愛的使者。

對蜜蜂和花朵而言，

奉獻快樂與接受快樂都是一種需要，也是極樂。

歐法里斯的人們啊，

要像花朵和蜜蜂一樣，沉醉在你們的快樂中。

And shall your flame or your smoke burden the wind?

Think you the spirit is a still pool which you can trouble with a staff?

Oftentimes in denying yourself pleasure you do but store the desire
in the recesses of your being.

Who knows but that which seems omitted today, waits for tomorrow?

Even your body knows its heritage and its rightful need
and will not be deceived.

And your body is the harp of your soul,

And it is yours to bring forth sweet music from it or confused sounds.

And now you ask in your heart, "How shall we distinguish that
which is good in pleasure from that which is not good?"

Go to your fields and your gardens, and you shall learn that it is the
pleasure of the bee to gather honey of the flower,

But it is also the pleasure of the flower to yield its honey to the bee.

For to the bee a flower is a fountain of life,

And to the flower a bee is a messenger of love,

And to both, bee and flower,

the giving and the receiving of pleasure is a need and an ecstasy.

People of Orphalese,

be in your pleasures like the flowers and the bees.

第25章

美

On Beauty

美不是一張乾渴的嘴，也不是一隻伸向前的空手，

而是一顆燃燒的心，一個迷醉的靈魂。

It is not a mouth thirsting nor an empty hand stretched forth.

But rather a heart inflamed and a soul enchanted.

　　　　個詩人說，跟我們說說「美」吧。

　　　　他回答：

你要到哪裡追尋美？

除非美就是你的道路，你的嚮導，

否則你如何找得到她？

除非美就是你言詞的編織者，

否則你如何能談論她？

委屈和受傷的人說：

「美是仁慈而溫柔的。

她走在我們之間，像個年輕的母親，為自己的光彩感到羞赧。」

熱情的人說：

「不，美是強大且令人害怕的東西，

她像暴風雨，

撼動我們腳下的大地，和頭頂上的天空。」

疲憊和厭倦的人說：

「美是柔聲軟語，

她在我們的性靈中說話。

她的聲音屈服於我們的沉默，

有如微弱的光，因害怕暗影而顫抖。」

And a poet said, "Speak to us of Beauty."
And he answered:

Where shall you seek beauty,
and how shall you find her
unless she herself be your way and your guide?
And how shall you speak of her
except she be the weaver of your speech?

The aggrieved and the injured say,
"Beauty is kind and gentle.
Like a young mother half-shy of her own glory she walks among us."

And the passionate say,
"Nay, beauty is a thing of might and dread.
"Like the tempest
she shakes the earth beneath us and the sky above us."

The tired and the weary say,
"Beauty is of soft whisperings.
She speaks in our spirit.
"Her voice yields to our silences
like a faint light that quivers in fear of the shadow."

但那些煩躁不安的人說：

「我們聽過她在群山之間呼喊，

然後蹄聲、振翅聲和獅吼聲

也隨著她的呼喊而來。」

夜晚，城裡的守夜人說：

「美將隨著東方的曙光升起。」

正午，辛勤工作的人和路上奔波的旅人說：

「我們看過她靠在夕陽的窗邊，

斜倚著大地。」

冬天，受困於冰雪的人說：

「她將隨著春天翻山越嶺而來。」

在酷暑中收割的人說：

「我們看見她和秋天的樹葉共舞，

也看到一片雪花飄落於她的髮際。」

這些都是你們所說的美。

但其實你們說的都不是美，而是未得到滿足的需要，

然而美不是需要，而是狂喜。

美不是一張乾渴的嘴，也不是一隻伸向前的空手，

而是一顆燃燒的心，一個迷醉的靈魂。

But the restless say,

"We have heard her shouting among the mountains,

"And with her cries came the sound of hoofs,

and the beating of wings and the roaring of lions."

At night the watchmen of the city say,

"Beauty shall rise with the dawn from the east."

And at noontide the toilers and the wayfarers say,

"We have seen her leaning over the earth

from the windows of the sunset."

In winter say the snow-bound,

"She shall come with the spring leaping upon the hills."

And in the summer heat the reapers say,

"We have seen her dancing with the autumn leaves,

and we saw a drift of snow in her hair."

All these things have you said of beauty,

Yet in truth you spoke not of her but of needs unsatisfied,

And beauty is not a need but an ecstasy.

It is not a mouth thirsting nor an empty hand stretched forth,

But rather a heart inflamed and a soul enchanted.

她不是你看見的形象，也不是你聽見的歌曲，

而是你閉上眼睛仍看得見的形象，

摀住耳朵仍聽得到的歌曲。

她不是粗皺樹皮底下的汁液，

也不是連接在利爪上的翅膀，

而是一座永遠盛開著花朵的花園，

和一群永遠在飛翔的天使。

歐里法斯的人們啊，

美是揭開面紗，露出聖潔面容的生命。

但你就是生命，你也是面紗。

美也是永恆，她凝視著鏡中的自己。

而你就是永恆，你也是鏡子。

It is not the image you would see nor the song you would hear,

But rather an image you see though you close your eyes

and a song you hear though you shut your ears.

It is not the sap within the furrowed bark,

nor a wing attached to a claw,

But rather a garden for ever in bloom

and a flock of angels for ever in flight.

People of Orphalese,

beauty is life when life unveils her holy face.

But you are life and you are the veil.

Beauty is eternity gazing at itself in a mirror.

But you are eternity and you are the mirror.

宗教

On Religion

如果你想要認識神，

就不要做解謎的人。

不如看看四周，

你將會看到祂在和你的孩子玩耍。

And if you would know God,

be not therefore a solver of riddles.

Rather look about you

and you shall see Him playing with your children.

<u>　　</u>個老祭司說，和我們講一講「宗教」吧。

　　他回答說：

今天我說的不都是宗教嗎？

宗教不就是所有的行為和反省？

宗教不也是那些既非行為，也非反省，

而是即使雙手忙著鑿刻石頭或織布時，

仍在靈魂中躍動的神奇與驚喜？

誰能將信仰和行為分開，

或是將信念和工作分開？

誰能將自己的時間攤在面前，

然後說，

「這些給神，這些給我自己；

這些給我的靈魂，其餘這些時間留給我的身體？」

你所有的時間都是在空中拍動的翅膀，從自己飛向自己。

把道德當作華服穿上身的人，不如光著身子。

風和太陽不會撕裂他的皮膚。

用倫理道德規範自己行為的人，

就是把他歌唱的鳥兒禁錮在籠中。

最自由的歌，在牢籠裡唱不出來。

And an old priest said, "Speak to us of Religion."
And he said:

Have I spoken this day of aught else?
Is not religion all deeds and all reflection,
And that which is neither deed nor reflection,
but a wonder and a surprise ever springing in the soul,
even while the hands hew the stone or tend the loom?

Who can separate his faith from his actions,
or his belief from his occupations?
Who can spread his hours before him,
saying,
"This for God and this for myself;
This for my soul and this other for my body?"
All your hours are wings that beat through space from self to self.

He who wears his morality but as his best garment were better naked.
The wind and the sun will tear no holes in his skin.
And he who defines his conduct by ethics
imprisons his songbird in a cage.
The freest song comes not through bars and wires.

還有人把敬神看作一扇窗，既能開也能關，
卻不曾探望自己的靈魂之屋，
那裡的窗戶可一直都是敞開的。

你每日的生活就是你的神殿，也是你的宗教。
不論你何時走進裡面，都要帶著你的一切，
帶著犁和熔爐，木槌和魯特琴，
帶著你為了需要或快樂而製造的東西，
因為在幻想中，你無法超越你的成就，
也無法跌落於你的失敗之下。
你還要帶著大家一起去：
因為在敬拜儀式中，你不會飛得比他們的希望更高，
也不會把自己貶到比他們的絕望更低。

如果你想要認識神，
就不要做解謎的人。
不如看看四周，
你將會看到祂在和你的孩子玩耍。
再看看天空，
你將會看到祂在雲中行走，在閃電中伸出雙臂，
然後隨著雨水落下。
你將會看見祂在花間微笑，
然後冉冉升上樹梢，在林中揮手。

And he to whom worshipping is a window, to open but also to shut,

has not yet visited the house of his soul whose windows are from

dawn to dawn.

Your daily life is your temple and your religion.

Whenever you enter into it take with you your all.

Take the plough and the forge and the mallet and the lute,

The things you have fashioned in necessity or for delight.

For in reverie you cannot rise above your achievements

nor fall lower than your failures.

And take with you all men:

For in adoration you cannot fly higher than their hopes

nor humble yourself lower than their despair.

And if you would know God,

be not therefore a solver of riddles.

Rather look about you

and you shall see Him playing with your children.

And look into space;

you shall see Him walking in the cloud, outstretching His arms in

the lightning and descending in rain.

You shall see Him smiling in flowers,

then rising and waving His hands in trees.

第 27 章

死亡

On Death

停止呼吸又是什麼？
不就是讓呼吸從永不止歇的潮汐中得到解脫，
使它能夠昇華，擴展，
且毫無窒礙地尋求神嗎？

And what is it to cease breathing
but to free the breath from its restless tides,
that it may rise and expand and seek God unencumbered?

接著艾蜜特拉說，現在我們想向您請教「死亡」。
於是他說：

你想知道死亡的祕密，

但除非你在生命的中心尋找，否則你怎麼找得到它？

貓頭鷹的視力只限於夜晚，白天是看不見的，

牠無法揭開光的神祕面紗。

倘若你真想看清死亡的精神，

就敞開你的心門，迎向生命的本質吧，

因為生命和死亡是一體的，

如同河流和海洋是一體的。

在你希望和欲念的深處，

存在著你對來世默然的了解，

猶如覆蓋於白雪之下懷著夢想的種子，

你的心靈也夢想著春天。

相信那些夢想吧，因為通往永恆的大門就隱藏在夢想中。

你對死亡的恐懼，就如同牧羊人站在國王面前禁不住顫抖，

因為國王即將用手輕觸他以表揚他。

那牧羊人顫抖之際，

心底難道不欣喜於自己將帶著國王的手印？

然而他為何更在意自己的顫抖？

T hen Almitra spoke, saying, "We would ask now of Death."
And he said:

You would know the secret of death.

But how shall you find it unless you seek it in the heart of life?

The owl whose night-bound eyes are blind unto the day cannot

unveil the mystery of light.

If you would indeed behold the spirit of death,

open your heart wide unto the body of life.

For life and death are one,

even as the river and the sea are one.

In the depth of your hopes and desires

lies your silent knowledge of the beyond;

And like seeds dreaming beneath the snow

your heart dreams of spring.

Trust the dreams, for in them is hidden the gate to eternity.

Your fear of death is but the trembling of the shepherd when he

stands before the king whose hand is to be laid upon him in honour.

Is the shepherd not joyful beneath his trembling,

that he shall wear the mark of the king?

Yet is he not more mindful of his trembling?

死亡不就是赤身露體站在風中，

在陽光下融化嗎？

停止呼吸又是什麼？

不就是讓呼吸從永不止歇的潮汐中得到解脫，

使它能夠昇華，擴展，且毫無窒礙地尋求神嗎？

只有等你喝過沉默之河的水，

你才能真正唱歌。

只有等你到達山頂，

你才會開始向上攀爬。

只有等到大地收回你的肢體，

你才能真正舞蹈。

For what is it to die but to stand naked in the wind

and to melt into the sun?

And what is it to cease breathing

but to free the breath from its restless tides,

that it may rise and expand and seek God unencumbered?

Only when you drink from the river of silence

shall you indeed sing.

And when you have reached the mountain top,

then you shall begin to climb.

And when the earth shall claim your limbs,

then shall you truly dance.

離別

The Farewell

我將隨風而去，

歐法里斯的人們啊，但我不會陷入虛無；

如果今天無法滿足你的需要和我的愛，

那麼就讓它成為承諾，直到另一天到來。

I go with the wind.

people of Orphalese, but not down into emptiness:

And if this day is not a fulfillment of your needs and my love,

then let it be a promise till another day.

現在已是傍晚時分。

女預言家艾蜜特拉說，

願今天、這個地方和你訴說智慧的心靈都受到祝福。

他回答，

說話的人是我嗎？我不也是個聆聽者嗎？

他走下神殿的階梯，

所有的人都跟隨著他。

他上了船，站在甲板上。

他再次面對人群，並且提高聲音說：

歐法里斯的人們啊，

風要我離開你們，

我雖然沒有風那麼匆忙，

但我也必須走了。

我們這些漂泊者啊，

總是尋找更孤寂的路，

從來不曾在度過一天的地方，開始新的一天；

也從來沒有在夕陽離開我們的地方，等待旭日升起。

即使大地沉睡了，我們仍在奔波。

我們是頑強的植物種子，

等我們身體成熟、心靈飽滿的時候，

就被送到微風跟前，吹散到各地。

A nd now it was evening.

And Almitra the seeress said,

"Blessed be this day and this place and your spirit that has spoken."

And he answered,

Was it I who spoke? Was I not also a listener?

Then he descended the steps of the Temple

and all the people followed him.

And he reached his ship and stood upon the deck.

And facing the people again, he raised his voice and said:

People of Orphalese,

the wind bids me leave you.

Less hasty am I than the wind,

yet I must go.

We wanderers,

ever seeking the lonelier way,

begin no day where we have ended another day;

and no sunrise finds us where sunset left us.

Even while the earth sleeps we travel.

We are the seeds of the tenacious plant,

and it is in our ripeness and our fullness of heart

that we are given to the wind and are scattered.

我和你們相處的時日短暫，

我說過的話更為簡短，

萬一我的聲音在你們的耳中漸漸微弱，

萬一我的愛在你們的記憶中漸漸消逝，

那時我會回來，

我會用更豐富的心，

更順從心靈的雙脣說話。

是的，我將隨著潮水歸來，

雖然死亡會掩蔽我，

深深的沉默會擁抱我，

但我仍然會再次尋求你們的了解，

而我的尋求將不會落空。

我說過的話若是真理，

那麼真理將以更清晰的聲音、

更貼近你思想的文字顯現出來。

我將隨風而去，

歐法里斯的人們啊，

但我不會陷入虛無；

如果今天無法滿足你的需要和我的愛，

那麼就讓它成為承諾，直到另一天到來。

Brief were my days among you,

and briefer still the words I have spoken.

But should my voice fade in your ears,

and my love vanish in your memory,

then I will come again,

And with a richer heart and lips more yielding to the spirit

will I speak.

Yea, I shall return with the tide,

And though death may hide me,

and the greater silence enfold me,

yet again will I seek your understanding.

And not in vain will I seek.

If aught I have said is truth,

that truth shall reveal itself in a clearer voice,

and in words more kin to your thoughts.

I go with the wind,

people of Orphalese,

but not down into emptiness;

And if this day is not a fulfillment of your needs and my love,

then let it be a promise till another day.

人的需求會變，

但他的愛不會變，

想以愛滿足需求的欲望也不會改變。

因此，你們要明白，我將會自深深的沉默中歸來。

晨霧消散於黎明時分，

只在田野之間留下露珠，

但它將再度升起，積聚成雲，然後落地為雨。

我也曾仿若那晨霧，

在闃然無聲的夜裡，走過你們的街道，

我的精神走進你們的住屋，

你們的心跳存在於我的心中，

你們的鼻息拂上我的臉龐，

我認識你們所有的人。

是啊，我知道你們的苦與樂，

在你們入睡時，你們的夢就是我的夢。

我經常與你們同在，好比群山環繞的湖泊，

我映照出你們心中的山巔和斜坡，

甚至映照出如同羊群一般，走過你們心頭的思想和欲念。

你們孩子的笑聲如小溪，年輕人的渴望如河水，

全都流入我沉默的湖水中。

Man's needs change,

but not his love,

nor his desire that his love should satisfy his needs.

Know, therefore, that from the greater silence I shall return.

The mist that drifts away at dawn,

leaving but dew in the fields,

shall rise and gather into a cloud and then fall down in rain.

And not unlike the mist have I been.

In the stillness of the night I have walked in your streets,

and my spirit has entered your houses,

And your heart-beats were in my heart,

and your breath was upon my face,

and I knew you all.

Aye, I knew your joy and your pain,

and in your sleep your dreams were my dreams.

And oftentimes I was among you a lake among the mountains.

I mirrored the summits in you and the bending slopes,

and even the passing flocks of your thoughts and your desires.

And to my silence came the laughter of your children in streams,

and the longing of your youths in rivers.

當小溪和河水沉降到我心深處，

它們仍未停止歌唱。

但比笑聲更甜蜜，比渴望更濃烈的感覺也奔向我。

那是你們內心的無窮無盡；

他是個巨人，你們不過是他的細胞和肌腱；

在他的吟唱中，你們的歌唱不過是無聲的悸動。

你們只有活在巨人裡面，才會遼闊；

我只有在注視他的時候，才看得見你們，並且愛你們。

因為若不是在他浩瀚的範圍裡，愛能走得多遠？

什麼樣的願景，什麼樣的期望，什麼樣的假設，

才能飛得比那片天空更高呢？

你們心中的巨人，

就像一株覆滿蘋果花的高大橡樹，

他的力量將你們與大地相連，

他的芳香使你們升向空中，

有了他的耐力，你們將永不凋亡。

有人告訴你們，

你們就像一條鎖鏈中最脆弱的環節一樣虛弱。

但這話只說對了一半，

因為你們也像最牢固的環節一樣堅固。

And when they reached my depth the streams and the rivers ceased

not yet to sing.

But sweeter still than laughter and greater than longing came to me.

It was the boundless in you;

The vast man in whom you are all but cells and sinews;

He in whose chant all your singing is but a soundless throbbing.

It is in the vast man that you are vast,

And in beholding him that I beheld you and loved you.

For what distances can love reach that are not in that vast sphere?

What visions, what expectations and what presumptions

can outsoar that flight?

Like a giant oak tree covered with apple blossoms

is the vast man in you.

His might binds you to the earth,

his fragrance lifts you into space,

and in his durability you are deathless.

You have been told that,

even like a chain, you are as weak as your weakest link.

This is but half the truth.

You are also as strong as your strongest link.

從你們最微小的行動去衡量你們，

就像是用大海中最脆弱的泡沫去揣想海洋的力量；

以你們的失敗評斷你們，

即是責怪四季的變幻無常。

是啊，你們就像大海，

雖然擱淺的船隻在你們的岸邊等待漲潮，

但如同海洋一樣，你無法催促潮汐。

你也像四季一樣，

雖然你在冬天時否定了春天，

但是在你體內蟄伏的春天，

卻在昏沉的睡意中微笑，沒有動氣。

不要以為我這麼說，是為了讓你們對彼此說：

「他在讚美我們，他只看見我們的好。」

我只不過是把你們已經知道的事說給你們聽。

以言語相傳的知識，

不就是無法言傳的知識的影子？

你的思想和我的言語，是從一個封閉的回憶盪漾出的波浪，

這份回憶記錄了我們的昨日，

也記錄了古代，那時大地尚不知有我們，也不知有自己。

這份回憶更記錄了大地尚混沌激盪時的漫漫長夜。

To measure you by your smallest deed is to reckon the power of ocean by the frailty of its foam.

To judge you by your failures is to cast blame upon the seasons for their inconstancy.

Aye, you are like an ocean,

And though heavy-grounded ships await the tide upon your shores,

yet, even like an ocean, you cannot hasten your tides.

And like the seasons you are also,

And though in your winter you deny your spring,

Yet spring, reposing within you,

smiles in her drowsiness and is not offended.

Think not I say these things in order that you may say the one to the other, "He praised us well. He saw but the good in us."

I only speak to you in words of that which you yourselves know in thought.

And what is word knowledge

but a shadow of wordless knowledge?

Your thoughts and my words are waves from a sealed memory

that keeps records of our yesterdays,

And of the ancient days when the earth knew not us nor herself,

And of nights when earth was upwrought with confusion.

智者來到你的面前，把他們的智慧傳授給你。

我則來到你的面前，想要得到你的智慧：

看哪，我找到比智慧更偉大的東西。

那就是你心中帶著的火焰精神，它越燒越旺；

而你，你不理會它的壯大，

卻為你的歲月凋零而哭泣。

只有追求肉體生命的人，才會懼怕墳墓。

這裡沒有墳墓，

這些山岳與平原是搖籃，也是踏腳石。

每當你們走過埋葬先人的田野，

仔細看看那裡吧，

你們便會看見自己和子女牽著手在跳舞。

確實，你們常常開心玩樂而不自知。

有些人來到你們面前，

憑藉著你們的信任，許下了黃金似的承諾，

你們則報以財富、權力和榮耀。

我給你們的算不上承諾，你們對我卻更是慷慨。

你們給了我對生命更深切的渴望。

而給一個人最可貴的禮物，

莫過於將他所有的目標變成乾渴的雙脣，

以及將他所有的生命化為泉水。

Wise men have come to you to give you of their wisdom.

I came to take of your wisdom:

And behold I have found that which is greater than wisdom.

It is a flame spirit in you ever gathering more of itself,

While you, heedless of its expansion,

bewail the withering of your days.

It is life in quest of life in bodies that fear the grave.

There are no graves here.

These mountains and plains are a cradle and a steppingstone.

Whenever you pass by the field where you have laid your ancestors

look well thereupon,

and you shall see yourselves and your children dancing hand in hand.

Verily you often make merry without knowing.

Others have come to you

to whom for golden promises made unto your faith

you have given but riches and power and glory.

Less than a promise have I given,

and yet more generous have you been to me.

You have given me my deeper thirsting after life.

Surely there is no greater gift to a man than that which turns all his

aims into parching lips and all life into a fountain.

我的榮耀和報酬就在這裡——

每當我找到生命之泉要暢飲的時候，

才發現那汩汩流動的水也是渴的；

我喝它時，它也在暢飲我。

你們有些人認為我驕傲，又過於羞澀，不肯接受禮物。

我的確驕傲，不肯接受俸祿，

但我不至於不接受禮物。

雖然你們希望我坐上你們的餐桌，

我卻在山裡吃著漿果；

雖然你們樂於收留我過夜，

我卻睡在神殿的門廊上。

然而，若非你們對我日夜的關懷，

我入嘴的食物怎會香甜？我入睡時又何來美夢圍繞？

為此，我要特別祝福你們：

你們惠我良多，自己卻渾然不知。

的確，一旦仁慈凝視著鏡中的自己，就會變成石頭；

而善行若以溫柔自詡，

即成為詛咒的根源。

你們有些人說我孤高，

說我沉醉於自己的孤獨；

And in this lies my honour and my reward, –

That whenever I come to the fountain to drink

I find the living water itself thirsty;

And it drinks me while I drink it.

Some of you have deemed me proud and over shy to receive gifts.

Too proud indeed am I to receive wages,

but not gifts.

And though I have eaten berries among the hills when you would

have had me sit at your board,

And slept in the portico of the temple when you would gladly have

sheltered me,

Yet was it not your loving mindfulness of my days and my nights that

made food sweet to my mouth and girdled my sleep with visions?

For this I bless you most:

You give much and know not that you give at all.

Verily the kindness that gazes upon itself in a mirror turns to stone,

And a good deed that calls itself by tender names

becomes the parent to a curse.

And some of you have called me aloof,

and drunk with my own aloneness,

你們也說：

「他和森林裡的樹木為伍，卻不與人來往。

他一個人坐在山頂，俯望我們的城市。」

的確，我曾登上高山，走過遙遠的地方。

可是，我若不是從很高很遠的地方眺望，

如何看得到你們？

我若不是走得夠遠，

如何能真正親近你們？

你們當中還有些人默默對我呼喊，

他們說：

「陌生人，陌生人，

喜歡站在高不可及之處的人，

你為何要住在老鷹築巢的山頂？

為何要尋找那找不著的東西？

你的網要捕捉什麼樣的暴風雨？

你想在空中獵捕何種如夢似幻的鳥？

來吧，和我們在一起。

下山吧，吃我們的麵包充飢，

喝我們的酒解渴。」

在他們靈魂的孤寂中，他們說了這些。

And you have said,

"He holds council with the trees of the forest, but not with men.

"He sits alone on hill-tops and looks down upon our city."

True it is that I have climbed the hills and walked in remote places.

How could I have seen you

save from a great height or a great distance?

How can one be indeed near

unless he be far?

And others among you called unto me, not in words,

and they said:

"Stranger, stranger,

lover of unreachable heights,

why dwell you among the summits where eagles build their nests?

"Why seek you the unattainable?

"What storms would you trap in your net,

"And what vaporous birds do you hunt in the sky?

"Come and be one of us.

"Descend and appease your hunger with our bread and quench your

thirst with our wine."

In the solitude of their souls they said these things;

但是，如果他們的孤寂更深，

就會懂得我尋找的，不過是你們快樂和痛苦的祕密；

我獵捕的，不過是你們那漫步在天際的大我。

不過，獵人也是獵物；

因為許多箭矢一飛離我的弓，便刺向我的胸膛。

而那天上飛的也是地上爬的；

因為我在陽光下展翅的時候，

落在地上的身影，竟是一隻烏龜。

我既是信徒，也是懷疑者；

因為我經常將手指探入我的傷口，

希望自己對你們更有信心，對你們更為了解。

就憑著這個信心和了解，我才說：

軀體局限不了你，

房屋和田地也圈不住你。

你們住在群山之上，

隨風漂泊。

你們不為取暖爬到陽光下，

也不為安全鑽進暗洞裡，

你們是自由的，

是擁抱大地、在天地之間游移的精靈。

But were their solitude deeper they would have known that I sought
but the secret of your joy and your pain,
And I hunted only your larger selves that walk the sky.

But the hunter was also the hunted;
For many of my arrows left my bow only to seek my own breast.
And the flier was also the creeper;
For when my wings were spread in the sun their shadow upon the
earth was a turtle.

And I the believer was also the doubter;
For often have I put my finger in my own wound that I might have
the greater belief in you and the greater knowledge of you.
And it is with this belief and this knowledge that I say,
You are not enclosed within your bodies,
nor confined to houses or fields.
That which is you dwells above the mountain
and roves with the wind.
It is not a thing that crawls into the sun for warmth or digs holes into
darkness for safety,
But a thing free,
a spirit that envelops the earth and moves in the ether.

如果這些話聽來含糊，

你們也不必試圖明白。

含糊與混沌是萬物之始，而非其終，

我寧可你們記得我是起始。

生命和一切生物皆孕育於迷霧中，

而不是水晶裡。

但誰又知道水晶不會是消散的迷霧呢？

我願你們在回憶我時記住這件事：

你們身上看似最柔弱、最迷惘的部分，

其實是最強健、最堅定的部分。

你們的骨骼結構，

難道不是靠你的氣息來支撐和強化的嗎？

你們建立的城市，和構成城市裡的一切，

難道不是源自你們已不復記憶的夢想嗎？

如果你們只看見氣息的起伏，

你們就看不見其他的一切；

如果你們能聽見夢的低語，

你們就聽不見其他的聲音。

但是，你們既看不見也聽不到，這樣也好。

If these be vague words,

then seek not to clear them.

Vague and nebulous is the beginning of all things, but not their end,

And I fain would have you remember me as a beginning.

Life, and all that lives,

is conceived in the mist and not in the crystal.

And who knows but a crystal is mist in decay?

This would I have you remember in remembering me:

That which seems most feeble and bewildered in you is the strongest and most determined.

Is it not your breath that has erected and hardened the structure of your bones?

And is it not a dream which none of you remember having dreamt, that built your city and fashioned all there is in it?

Could you but see the tides of that breath

you would cease to see all else,

And if you could hear the whispering of the dream

you would hear no other sound.

But you do not see, nor do you hear, and it is well.

蒙著你雙眼的面紗，

將由編織它的那雙手掀開；

塞住你耳朵的黏土，

也將由揉捏它的手指戳穿。

於是你將看見，

於是你將聽到，

但你不要哀嘆曾經目盲，

也不要後悔曾經耳聾。

因為那一天，你將會明白，冥冥中萬物皆有其目的。

你將會讚美黑暗，如同你讚美光明。

說完這些話，他舉目四顧，

看到他船上的舵手站在船舵旁邊，

時而凝視張滿的船帆，時而遙望遠方。

他說：

我的船長很有耐心，他太有耐心。

風兒起，帆飄揚，

就連方向舵也在乞求指引方向；

然而我的船長卻靜靜等待我沉默下來。

我的水手們啊，

他們聽過偉大海洋的合唱，

也曾耐心聽我說話。

The veil that clouds your eyes

shall be lifted by the hands that wove it,

And the clay that fills your ears

shall be pierced by those fingers that kneaded it.

And you shall see.

And you shall hear.

Yet you shall not deplore having known blindness,

nor regret having been deaf.

For in that day you shall know the hidden purposes in all things,

And you shall bless darkness as you would bless light.

After saying these things he looked about him,

and he saw the pilot of his ship standing by the helm

and gazing now at the full sails and now at the distance.

And he said:

Patient, over patient, is the captain of my ship.

The wind blows, and restless are the sails;

Even the rudder begs direction;

Yet quietly my captain awaits my silence.

And these my mariners,

who have heard the choir of the greater sea,

they too have heard me patiently.

現在，他們不用再等了。

我已準備就緒。

溪流已奔入大海，

偉大的母親將再次擁兒子入懷。

別了，歐法里斯的人們，

這一天已經結束。

暮色漸漸向我們收攏，如同睡蓮漸漸閉合自己的明天。

我們在這裡得到的東西都將保存下來；

如果這些不夠，

我們就必須再聚，

一起向施予者伸手乞求。

別忘了，我將會回到你們身邊。

再過些時候，

我的渴望就會積聚塵土和泡沫，成為另一副軀體。

再過些時候，在風上歇息片刻之後，

另一個女人會孕育我。

別了，各位，還有我和你們共度的青春歲月。

我們在夢中相識，也不過是昨天的事。

我孤獨的時候，你們唱歌給我聽；

你們渴望之際，我也曾搭起空中的高塔。

Now they shall wait no longer.

I am ready.

The stream has reached the sea,

and once more the great mother holds her son against her breast.

Fare you well, people of Orphalese.

This day has ended.

It is closing upon us even as the water-lily upon its own tomorrow.

What was given us here we shall keep,

And if it suffices not,

then again must we come together and together stretch our hands

unto the giver.

Forget not that I shall come back to you.

A little while,

and my longing shall gather dust and foam for another body.

A little while, a moment of rest upon the wind,

and another woman shall bear me.

Farewell to you and the youth I have spent with you.

It was but yesterday we met in a dream.

You have sung to me in my aloneness,

and I of your longings have built a tower in the sky.

然而，如今我們的睡眠已經遁逃，我們的夢想已到盡頭，
黎明也不再。
日正當中，昏沉欲睡的我們已然清醒，
我們必須別離。
倘若我們能在記憶的垂暮時分重逢，
我們將再交談，你們也將再為我唱一首更深沉的歌；
倘若我們的雙手能在另一個夢中交握，
我們將在空中搭起另一座高塔。

說著說著，他向水手做了個手勢，
於是他們立刻起錨解纜，
船離開停泊處，航向東方。
人群發出一聲哭喊，彷彿發自同一顆心，
那哭喊響徹暮色，傳到海上，
宛如洪亮的號角聲。
只有愛蜜特拉默默凝望著船，
直到它消失於霧中。
所有人皆散去之後，她仍然獨自站在海堤上，
心中惦念著他說的話：

「再過些時候，
在風上歇息片刻之後，
另一個女人會孕育我。」

But now our sleep has fled and our dream is over,

and it is no longer dawn.

The noontide is upon us and our half waking has turned to fuller day,

and we must part.

If in the twilight of memory we should meet once more,

we shall speak again together and you shall sing to me a deeper song.

And if our hands should meet in another dream we shall build

another tower in the sky.

So saying he made a signal to the seamen,

and straightaway they weighed anchor and cast the ship loose from

its moorings, and they moved eastward.

And a cry came from the people as from a single heart,

and it rose into the dusk and was carried out over the sea

like a great trumpeting.

Only Almitra was silent,

gazing after the ship until it had vanished into the mist.

And when all the people were dispersed she still stood alone upon

the sea-wall, remembering in her heart his saying:

"A little while,

a moment of rest upon the wind,

and another woman shall bear me."

國家圖書館出版品預行編目 (CIP) 資料

先知：公視影集《你的孩子不是你的孩子》朗
誦詩篇原典，綻放愛與哲思之美的不朽散文詩
集【中英對照‧絕美精裝版】／卡里‧紀伯倫
(Kahlil Gibran) 作；趙永芬譯 .-- 三版 .-- 新北市
：野人文化出版：遠足文化發行，2020.03
　　面；　公分
中英對照
譯自：The prophet
ISBN 978-986-384-419-8(精裝)

865.751　　　　　　　　　　　　　　109002050

先知

線上讀者回函專用 QR CODE，您的
寶貴意見，將是我們進步的最大動力。

Golden Age 24

先知

公視影集《你的孩子不是你的孩子》朗
誦詩篇原典，綻放愛與哲思之美的不朽
散文詩集【中英對照‧絕美精裝版】

作　　者	卡里‧紀伯倫（Kahlil Gibran）
譯　　者	趙永芬

野人文化股份有限公司

社　　長	張瑩瑩
總 編 輯	蔡麗真
責任編輯	陳瑾璇
行銷企劃	林麗紅
封面設計	莊謹銘
內頁排版	洪素貞

出　　版	野人文化股份有限公司
發　　行	遠足文化事業股份有限公司（讀書共和國出版集團）
	地址：231新北市新店區民權路108-2號9樓
	電話：（02）2218-1417　傳真：（02）8667-1065
	電子信箱：service@bookrep.com.tw
	網址：www.bookrep.com.tw
	郵撥帳號：19504465遠足文化事業股份有限公司
	客服專線：0800-221-029
法律顧問	華洋法律事務所　蘇文生律師
印　　製	呈靖印刷股份有限公司
初版首刷	2017年05月
二版首刷	2018年06月
三版首刷	2020年03月
三版五刷	2024年01月

有著作權　侵害必究
特別聲明：有關本書中的言論內容，不代表本公司/出版集團之立場與意見，
文責由作者自行承擔
歡迎團體訂購，另有優惠，請洽業務部（02）22181417分機1124

書　名 _____

姓　名 _____ □女 □男　年齡 _____

地　址 _____
　　　 _____

電　話 _____　手機 _____

Email _____

□同意 □不同意　　收到野人文化新書電子報

學　歷 □國中(含以下) □高中職　□大專　　□研究所以上
職　業 □生產/製造 □金融/商業 □傳播/廣告 □軍警/公務員
　　　 □教育/文化 □旅遊/運輸 □醫療/保健 □仲介/服務
　　　 □學生　　 □自由/家管 □其他

◆你從何處知道此書？
　□書店：名稱 _____　□網路：名稱 _____
　□量販店：名稱 _____　□其他 _____

◆你以何種方式購買本書？
　□誠品書店　□誠品網路書店　□金石堂書店　□金石堂網路書店
　□博客來網路書店　□其他 _____

◆你的閱讀習慣：
　□親子教養　□文學 □翻譯小說 □日文小說 □華文小說 □藝術設計
　□人文社科　□自然科學　□商業理財　□宗教哲學 □心理勵志
　□休閒生活（旅遊、瘦身、美容、園藝等）　□手工藝／DIY □飲食／食譜
　□健康養生　□兩性　□圖文書／漫畫 □其他 _____

◆你對本書的評價：（請填代號，1.非常滿意　2.滿意　3.尚可　4.待改進）
　書名 _____ 封面設計 _____ 版面編排 _____ 印刷 _____ 內容 _____
　整體評價 _____

◆你對本書的建議：_____
　_____
　_____

23141
新北市新店區民權路108-2號9樓
野人文化股份有限公司 收

請沿線撕下對折寄回

野人

書號：0NGA6024

延伸閱讀

生如夏花・泰戈爾新月集 & 漂鳥集

【中英對照｜絕美精裝版】

復刻印度名家彩色插畫｜譯者導讀泰戈爾生平與作品
Stray birds & The Crescent Moon

★諾貝爾文學獎得主泰戈爾畢生經典之作
★ 325 首哲思格言《漂鳥集》+40 首純真長詩《新月集》＝
　 365 個平凡日常的心靈綠洲

｜**自然生死**｜使生如夏花之絢爛，死如秋葉之靜美。
｜**愛戀纏綿**｜世界對著它的情人，揭下浩瀚的面具。
　　　　　　　它縮小，小如一首歌，小如一枚永恆的吻。
｜**哲思天命**｜我們錯看世界，反說它欺騙我們。
｜**世間孤寂**｜人走進喧鬧的人群，只為淹沒他沉默的呼喊。

茶花女

文學史上三大青春悲戀小說，小仲馬成名代表作

La dame aux camélias

★獨家收錄《茶花女》文學沙龍特輯
★法文直譯精裝版

家境貧苦的瑪格麗特，憑藉著天生麗質，搖身一變成為巴黎
貴族爭相討好的交際花，可是在那浮靡的亮麗背後，蘊藏了
一個女孩渴求心靈伴侶的簡單願望。當她邂逅了富家公子阿
爾芒之後，一切有了轉變的契機。然而阿爾芒父親的意外來
訪，迫使她面臨現實的殘酷無情。為了阿爾芒的前途、為了
另一位純潔女孩的幸福，她決心作出此生最偉大的舉動……